EYES IN THE DUST

AND OTHER STORIES

DAVID PEAK

This is a work of fiction. All of the characters, names, incidents, organizations, and dialogue in this novel are either the products of the author's imagination or are used fictitiously.

The views expressed in this work are solely those of the authors and do not necessarily reflect the views of the publisher, and the publisher hereby disclaims any responsibility for them.

ISBN: 978-1-950305-62-9 (sc)
ISBN: 978-1-950305-63-6 (ebook)
Library of Congress Control Number: 2020937709

First printing edition: April 2, 2021
Published by Trepidatio Publishing in the United States of America.
Cover Design and Layout: Don Noble / Rooster Republic Press
Edited by Sean Leonard
Proofreading and Interior Layout by Scarlett R. Algee

Trepidatio Publishing, an imprint of JournalStone Publishing
3205 Sassafras Trail
Carbondale, Illinois 62901

Trepidatio books may be ordered through booksellers or by contacting:
JournalStone | www.journalstone.com

CONTENTS

EYES IN THE DUST

AND OTHER STORIES

INTRODUCTION

PUMPED UP ON ADRENALINE after returning from a hunting trip, best friends J and D pointed their rifles at each other. Screwing around in J's grandmother's living room, working their weapon's action and pretending to shoot at each other, D didn't realize his gun was loaded. He pulled the trigger and shot J through the jaw into his neck. J died instantly.

It was the summer of 1985. We'd just returned to school in August when talk of J's death spread around junior high. My locker used to be next to theirs. We'd nothing in common. My English teacher (her name escapes me) cried in class when she broke the news. I don't remember details; I was too busy drawing occult symbols and lyrics to Celtic Frost songs on my Pee-Chee folder, trying to block out the sense of chaotic sorrow of which I couldn't fully empathize. It worried me then. It worries me thirty-five years later.

I went to the auditorium for the school's memorial service because it meant I could skip classes for the rest of the day. "Stairway to Heaven" played over the sound system. I'd wanted to escape that small podunk town in the Pacific Northwest for years, but sitting there made me want to run away that very instant. I wondered where D and his family moved to after J died. I wondered why the commiseration I felt was a monotone gray, almost innocuous in its presence.

What is the appeal, if any, of unpleasant storytelling? What allure in the dreary? My anecdote above doesn't have any supernatural elements. Real life isn't magical. Most pop-culture horror is escapist wishful thinking, fantasies darkened by gouts of gore and notions of the esoteric, typically Western conceits such as monotheistic traditions or theosophy or other nonsense, horrors that attempt to evoke discomfort because that's what's expected. Horror leans conservative. This is how it's always been. A cultural twitch, hereditary nerve spasm. Horror argues that the world would be so much better if the fantastic were real because that's what has always been known—established traditions regarding the uneasy separation between the physical and nonphysical. If were-things slavered, pyrokinetic children wreaked havoc, vampires flitted, and gods schemed within the ticky-tacky structures of this universe, living would be that much more worthwhile. Things used to be better when gods judged and ghosts haunted.

Except things never were better. The world has always been an abattoir in which stability is achieved when your hooves gain solid footing on blood-slick concrete. To say it's an apathetic universe has become something of a cliché. Why would an uncaring cosmos be a revelation? Anna Kavan said it far better than I: "Real life is a hateful and tiresome dream" and existence is "just a nightmare and the universe has no meaning." There are no angels to protect your back, and even the most pious knows it in their heart of hearts, buried deep beneath eschatological compost and failed dreams. We are well aware that it's an eternity of drudgery, so why get worked up over it?

Writers like Peak get worked up about it because there's liberation in that thought. Freedom from the tyranny of meaning. Peak gets it. Now, this isn't to say he avoids the violation of accepted constructs, or excludes anything that might be called supernatural, it's just that when he does, the weirdness coalesces into some strange new species not yet identified. When the uncanny occurs in a Peak tale, it's an unsettling *magic* that is more companion to nihilism and pessimism than the banal comforts of pentagrams or haunts or witches or psychics. His horrors are anything but the staid tried and true the vast majority of dark fiction reflects. He creates an enthralling misery by acknowledging how dreadful it is to *be*.

Take the stories "Helping Hands" and "King of the Rats." Both proceed with crisp, precise prose; both eschew the paranormal as a source of frisson; both are philosophically pessimistic, as distinct from misanthropic. But there's grim spirituality to be found in the gut-shot visceral, in the ugliness of slaughtered cows and condescending white-savior tropes. These horrors aren't escapist fun, no more than, say, Hubert Selby's depictions of the banality of violence or the democratic nature of cruelty. Uncompromising storytelling can all too often fall into angst-ridden clichés or edgy posturing—suffice it to say, Peak is far too skilled to allow this to happen. His stories offer the transcendental in the cognizable.

After finishing "The Gutter at the Bottom of the World," set in the San Fernando Valley, an area that encompasses both the wealthiest and most run-down neighborhoods in California, a place where "...things were almost always as bad as feared..." I felt as if I'd just read a sleazy panic attack. It left a greasy film on my brain. The only other time I'd felt that way was reading Ramsey Campbell's masterpiece, *The Grin of the Dark*. Higher praise I cannot give. Similarly, an unsettling encroachment of paranoia runs through "Strange Signals from the Center of the Earth." It's uncomfortably resonant. "House of Abjection" is also heavy with atmosphere, leaving a queasy memory residue behind. All of Peak's stories are thick with setting. Again and again he conjures an elusive magical substance that occurs when pessimistic philosophies and compelling characters are dissolved into ambience. A mad alchemist, his writing is rare alchemy.

A childhood friend was playing by himself in an open field where people illegally dumped their shit. He came across a battered, old Porta Potty. Its door was missing. The tank was cracked open. The waste had coagulated into a mushy boulder. Inside, he saw an object wrapped in duct tape. Being an inquisitive eight year old, he held his breath and retrieved the bundle. It took some effort, but he managed to tear a portion of the tape away. It was the corpse of a newborn.

He swore the body still felt warm. That may have been due to the activity of anaerobic bacteria. I don't know. It was long ago. What wonders that infant must have seen as someone, presumably a loved one, bound it in sticky strips. What fantastic vistas it must have gazed upon, its brain unable to process what it was experiencing—even if said brain had still been developing. I don't know, of course.

They never found the dead baby's mother. As far as my childhood friend remembers, nobody was ever a suspect and the investigation went nowhere.

Peak understands that all the misanthropy in the universe still necessitates a human presence. All colloquies require a human brain to experience the tale, whether writer or reader. Storytelling presents a sort of "observer effect," during which the observation of said tale has an effect on the story depending on the reader's interpretation, and the story has an effect on the reader, altering their superposition state. As trite as it sounds, we invent meaning from whole cloth by telling stories. Pattern-seeking primates tell stories invented inside brains that can only decipher thin peels of reality.

So we pretend. Contrive purpose. Every aspect of this *place* is doomed, destined for nothing of any particular value. Peak finds a sort of grandeur in exalting the arbitrary churnings of this engine, or what Mathilde Blind termed the "hectic beauty of decay" in her poem "The Evening of the Year." Dung beetles tirelessly roll feces into orbs while

Pteriidae form pearls around parasitic invaders. Arduous labor is no less impressive when the results are not life affirming or beautiful. The planet is a wobbly clot in the artery of space, and this itself offers a bleak affirmation.

Cosmic epistemology is truly unknowable, so we stick a needle into our veins and inject something that makes us dream of better places. Of places far away, unafflicted by the sick disorientation of stories such as "The Final Diagnosis of Doctor Lazare," a particularly potent tale with an Aickmanesque ambiguity laced with cosmic uncertainty and something else far more malicious bubbling underneath. Similarly, "Eyes in the Dust," a prolonged nightmare of grief, hints at what could be interpreted as panpsychism or object-oriented ontology, all marching to an inevitable demise. Peak doesn't hold the reader by the hand. He requires them to pay attention, derive importance from action. A kind of kinetic epistemology within the writing, not a thought-balloon explanation dangled over a character's head.

But I won't comment on every story here. I've no business writing introductions, much less imposing my interpretations of stories. All I can do is emphasize my admiration for Peak's work. *Eyes in the Dust and Other Stories* takes me back to my roots, cleaves through to the bone. Though geographically distinct from my childhood, this collection evokes Breece D'J Pancake and *The River's Edge* and Ann Quin's notion that "What we all want is some contact to make us feel that we do exist, because beyond that, there is a complete sort of void," as well as Jayne Anne Phillips's "dirty realism" and the swooningly romantic nihilism of Ligotti's cocktail of hyperreality and Catholic hysteria and—

All of this is just me spit-balling. Trotting out decades' old whiffs of familiarity as references. Childhood influences. Save points on an old video game. But Peak is his own thing. Reading this book is like removing duct tape from a corpse's head. The face remains miraculously pristine. It has no eyes, but it can still see. A thing molded from mud and tape, Sherwood Anderson's "grotesque little god with a twisted face" brought to fruition. Riverbeds where "ancients handed down memorized stories to their young." Peak brings to mind John Hawkes's dark futility, of miserable lives trotted out in pointless predictability. Life unrelentingly racing to nothing at all.

What poetry to be found in hopelessness?

The world was never pristine. It never will be. But we tell stories anyway, pretending, hoping that one day we might experience something flawless. Achieve something near perfection. Glimpse a face that suggests a modicum of sympathy in the decades we're afforded to sing, to fuck, to experiment with drugs, to be a dumb fifteen-year-old kid shoving the barrel of a gun in your buddy's face or to shoot dumb cattle to stave off boredom. We dream of cosmic consolations, and do so wholly aware that we have to pretend all of this is worthwhile as we plod along. But we are assured nothing other than an end in ink-black sludge within a Porta Potty. Maybe we'll be remembered that way.

Peak reminds us to keep at it. Go through the motions in the hell of good intentions. Keep swimming through dark muck to unseen shores. Go on in hopes we can someday escape this podunk town in this podunk universe.

Even if we all know there's no hope in hell of ever getting away from here.

Christopher Slatsky
Los Angeles, California
January, 2021

HELPING HANDS

MALMOUD, THE VILLAGE LEADER, grabbed Betsy by the hand, the loose skin on his thin arm purple beneath the white glare of the sun. His head was covered in thick shocks of white hair, his obsidian eyes sunk deep in their sockets.

He'd been hovering around her ever since she'd climbed down from Brian's mud-caked Jeep, tilting his head back and forth as he eyed her blond ponytail, her neatly pressed safari pants.

He jerked Betsy's arm as he pulled her through the small, nameless village outside Wau in West Bahr al Ghazal.

These villages were popping up everywhere in South Sudan, everywhere in sub-Saharan Africa for that matter, as quickly and haphazardly as dust settling after a storm.

The landscape of South Sudan is bleak—the land of biblical cataclysm, of annual droughts giving way to annual floods. The sky is always full of birds of prey: buzzards, eagles, kites.

Malmoud kept turning around, kept saying something in his language—Thuongjang, the Dinka language, the language of the Nile—but it was incomprehensible to Betsy's ears, too rich in vowels, too formless, too breathy. *Brian would know what he's saying,* she thought. *Brian speaks six languages.*

It's nearly impossible for an American to visit South Sudan without a chaperone. Betsy found Brian online. At twenty-seven, he was already working on his doctorate in anthropology. He had a ruddy face and bright eyes. He worked for the International Rescue Committee. She emailed him and he responded. She only had to pay him $450.

Malmoud's teeth flashed yellow in his wide mouth, his tongue a vibrant pink, eyes radiating anger. He wore nothing except a pair of faded camouflage cutoffs.

They passed by small huts made of grass, "thuckles" they called them. They passed by houses of rusted green and yellow sheet metal. They passed by huts made from dried mud, sagging tin roofs stretched overhead, huts made from rotting wood, chicken-wire fences strung alongside the dirt path that wound through the center of the village.

There was no electricity, no running water, no telephones. Brian told Betsy that some of these people had satellite phones, but so far she hadn't seen any.

The sky was a blue dome, cloudless, stretching endlessly, as large as the world itself.

She was struck by the silence of this place, the emptiness. A biplane buzzed in the sky, somewhere in the distance. Betsy made a visor with her hand and looked into the sun.

Malmoud pulled at her once more, muttered something in his strange language, nodded his head toward the International Rescue Committee tent. He let go of her hand. Betsy felt his sweat cooling in her palm. He side-stepped behind her, touched the small of her back, and using the tips of his fingers, gave her a light push.

Betsy looked down. The dirt in front of the tent had been kicked up, trampled, as if a hundred people had passed through the entrance that morning.

"You go," he said, his tongue struggling over the sharp angles of English consonants. "Look inside."

The entrance of the tent was a dark slit between two flaps of canvas, red crosses in white circles painted on either side. Betsy looked around for Brian, for any of the IRC workers, and saw nothing but dark faces peeking out from behind huts, from within thuckles.

The biplane's high-pitched buzzing was louder now, approaching the village.

"Go," Malmoud said. "Now."

Betsy felt the old man's eyes boring into her, hotter than the sun. She'd only been here—here in this nameless village—for ten minutes. She'd only left Kenya that morning.

She took a step forward and grabbed hold of one of the canvas flaps, pulled it back, and looked inside.

***

"There was a pile of arms," Betsy said. "Maybe twelve of them, twelve individual arms, stacked like chicken bones, pools of blood all over the place.

"In the back of the tent, all huddled together, there were dead children—no older than eight or nine. They'd bled to death. Their lips had turned gray, puckered up against their faces. Their eyes were still open, crawling with flies. The stench—*my God*—the stench was unbelievable." She paused. "They were the only kids in the entire village. After that...that was it. There were no children left."

She was home now, back in Farmington Hills, Michigan. She'd arrived early that morning, taken a cab home, climbed the stairs, and fallen into a long nap. Paul, her fiancé, had woken her just after sundown, roused her gently by stroking the side of her face with the backs of his fingers. He was nearly done with dinner, he said. He was sorry for waking her.

He hadn't said anything about her early return, hadn't asked her any questions. *He knows I'll tell him when I'm ready,* Betsy thought as she slid out of bed.

She set the table for dinner. It was covered in an elegant, white cloth. The lights were dimmed. The windows were open. The humid summer air smelled like trees.

The sight of wood floors, polished and clean, of floral-print wallpaper, track lighting—these things comforted Betsy in a way she would have never thought possible.

Paul was washing the dishes. They'd been engaged for nearly a year. Betsy's trip to Africa was something they had both agreed she needed to do, something she needed to get out of the way before they settled down, started their family. Three months overseas and then it would be time to start a family.

As Betsy told her story, he occasionally responded, his voice muffled beneath the sound of running water. He sounded uncomfortable, like he didn't know quite what to say.

"They'd been hacked off at the shoulder," she said, shutting the cabinet door, holding a plate beneath each arm, a glass in each hand, her hard-earned waitressing skills at work. "It was still there, next to the pile of arms. The machete. Its blade was nicked, covered in dried blood."

Three days had passed. She'd taken the first available flight home, a full month earlier than she'd planned. She lost the will to help, had never been able to go birding in Botswana like she'd wanted. All the way home, all she'd been able to think about were the birds in Botswana. They were supposed to be the most beautiful in the world.

All she remembered were the buzzards and the kites in Sudan.

"These people actually cut off the arms of their children. All because they didn't know what an *inoculation* was—what *vaccines* were. We found out later, we learned that they thought we'd been injecting them with poison. That's what Malmoud said. You should have seen the look on his face. Those villagers, they nearly killed those IRC people. And I don't know why, for some reason they thought I was there to help. They thought I could bring their children back to life. Like I was magic."

Betsy set the glasses on the table, then the plates. She picked up a box of matches and lit the candles. A gust of summer wind blew in through the open windows. The flames jumped but held strong.

"I know I was told, 'Don't expect to make things better.' That's what Brian said when I first got there—to Sudan. 'Don't think that just because you come from privilege that you can change things.' The great white savior. It's the wrong attitude. But I never thought it was going to be like that. Christ, I don't know how we're supposed to wipe out polio if..." Betsy's voice faltered in her throat.

Paul stood in the doorway, drying his hands on a dishrag. The sleeves of his shirt were rolled up to his elbows. He was a handsome man with a strong jaw and dark eyes. Something about the way he stood there reminded Betsy how much she loved him.

"Jesus," he said, coming toward her. "Why didn't you tell me?" He gently slid his hand around the back of her neck, wrapped his other arm around her lower back. He pulled her close. She loved this. She loved being held like this. It made her feel safe.

"I had no idea," he said. "I had no idea you were living with this."

Betsy angled her chin upward, smelled the wine on Paul's breath as he came in close and spoke softly in her ear. His skin smelled of soap. He said everything she expected. *It's okay. There's nothing to worry about. You did all you could. You're a good person. Those people need the guiding light.*

They never got around to eating that night. Instead they sat on the couch in the living room, finished two bottles of red wine. They talked until two in the morning. By the time they went to sleep, Betsy's eyes were swollen from crying. As they climbed the stairs, she felt nauseated. *Only the wine,* she thought. Paul held her around the waist, supporting her. Her legs were rubbery and she had to hold onto the handrail. *In the morning I'll feel better.*

* * *

Insects filled her dreams. Gnats. Mosquitoes. Dragonflies. Praying mantises. They were the size of cars. They swooped down upon her, emerged from endless black skies, flapping their monstrous wings.

Their eyes were like silver domes. She saw herself reflected in their eyes. She saw hundreds of versions of herself, small, terrified. She saw her face bent into new angles.

She covered her face with her arms. She was running in the desert. Somehow she knew it was the Sahara. Her feet were bare, the sand lunar gray, cold, the sky a black void. The insects droned from somewhere above her, beyond her vision.

In the distance she saw the IRC tent bathed in moonlight, recognized the bright red crosses on the entrance. And then she was there, pulling back the canvas flaps. Now there was silence. The insects were gone. She took a step inside the tent.

She felt herself quickly sinking into a warm pool of blood. It closed around her knees. It sucked her down like a mouth. Then it was at her waist, smelling like copper. She held her arms in the air and tried to scream. She couldn't make a noise. It licked at her armpits. She struggled, and for a second she thought she might break free. Then she slid down even farther and the blood filled her mouth. She tried to scream again and felt it pouring down her throat, into her lungs, her stomach, until it filled her up completely.

* * *

Time passed. Two, three days. Betsy got the flu. Every morning, she woke up, darted to the bathroom, and threw up bilious acid. The walls spun around her.

She thought of all the shots the government made her get before she could go to Africa: Hepatitis A, Hepatitis B, Meningitis, Rabies, Typhoid, Tetanus-Diptheria, Measles, Polio. She thought of all the paperwork she'd signed, all of the documentation.

She stayed in bed all day. Her eyelids twitched with dreams.

When Paul came home from work, he served her plain foods on a tray. He served her chicken broth and unbuttered toast. He served her Jell-O cut into little cubes. She wouldn't touch any of it. Finally he started giving her bowls of ice chips, told her—begged her—to hold them in her mouth. He gave her water, glass after glass after glass of water.

She had nothing but time, nothing to do but think. She did her best to remember what happened in Wau. She thought of what happened after she saw the arms, the children.

The biplane's buzzing turned into a roar as it approached the village, swooping over the huts in a wide arc before touching down in the dry, surrounding fields.

Betsy emerged from the darkness of the tent and fell to her knees, then to her hands. The dirt was dry and hot against her palms. Her stomach pulled inward and she dry heaved, hard enough to break the blood vessels around her eyes. A thin cry escaped her mouth, one she didn't recognize, an animal lowing. Malmoud stood over her, yelling. He stomped back and forth, bringing his knees up high, slamming his feet into the dirt.

She heard Brian's voice, down the footpath, a hundred yards away. He was arguing with somebody.

Next thing she knew she was in the back of Brian's Jeep and they were about to cross the border back into Kenya.

The sun was relentless. The land around them was flat and brown.

They approached the border, nothing more than a small shack, a barricade built of yellow two-by-fours. A dozen men—young boys, really—in mismatched, baggy camouflage uniforms stopped them. They appeared unsure of what to do. They rifled aimlessly through their bags. They argued with Brian.

There was a small metal sign on a post with a message written in Kishwahili, English, and Arabic. The sign warned of taking photographs, said it was a criminal offense.

The guards had AK-47s. They held them at their hips, posed with them. They had meanness in their eyes. Betsy had never seen anything like it. These kids reminded her of abused dogs.

"*American*," Brian said. And then he reverted back to words that Betsy could not understand.

The boys let them go soon after that. It wasn't until the Jeep bounced along the dusty road into Lokichokio that Brian started talking. And then once he started, he couldn't stop.

"Don't worry," he said, checking the rearview mirrors. "The IRC workers got out of there as soon as they realized what was happening, as soon as they figured out the kids had been rounded up.

"Malmoud—that old man—he was the one. He was the one who did it. Did you go in the tent? Did you see what was in there? Christ, I never should have let you go with him. Somebody—I don't know who, must've been one of the IRC workers—somebody put out a dispatch, I don't even know who to. That plane, it was two human-rights defenders, Americans. None of us knew what to do. We were yelling, we were all scared, panicked. They were going to kill us all. That's when I found you." He kept going like that. She couldn't understand anything he said.

It wasn't until she was on a plane, flying out of Nairobi, that Betsy cried.

* * *

One morning Betsy woke up, got out of bed, and felt her legs give out beneath her. Her bones pulled her straight down. First her elbow smacked against the hard wood floor, then her hips. A wavering cry escaped her throat—that same one from the village—the feeling of sand hot against her palms. Icy fear coursed through her body. Her fingertips tingled.

She soldier-crawled her way to the bathroom, sat against the tub, looked at her feet. Her vision was blurry. It took a few seconds before things came into focus.

Crooked columns of sunlight poured in through the small window next to the toilet, illuminating bits of dust that danced in the air.

The skin of her toes had turned black. It looked like her skin had shrunk over the bones in her foot. Her toenails were a wan pink. The cuticles had turned orange, like they'd been stained with iodine. The bridge of her foot was beet red, covered in open sores that glistened white in the light.

Betsy's heart pounded as she inspected her feet. She thought of words like *gangrene*, *necrotic*, *fetid*.

She looked at her hands. Her palms were covered in sores. The skin on her fingers was so black it was shiny, almost blue.

She was too tired to do anything. She was too tired to crawl back into the bedroom, to lift herself up to the phone, too tired to dial numbers, to explain who she was, where she was, what was wrong. She was too tired to ask for help.

Fuzzy warmth swirled behind her eyes. She let herself go down into the warm mouth of the blood. *Paul will find me*, she thought. *Paul will find me and Paul will help.*

* * *

She was in a white bed. The bed's frame was metal and painted white. The white sheets were tucked tightly over her body, but her body was not there. Her arms were tucked beneath the sheets, but her arms were not there. Her legs and feet did not push against the sheet.

She was back in the Sahara, surrounded by the cold, lunar sands. The sky was black. There were no stars. There was moonlight on everything but there was no moon.

A giant mosquito was perched at the foot of the bed, clinging to the ornate footboard, all six of its massive, pipe-cleaner legs holding the footboard like a buzzard holds the branch of a tree. Its legs bent out at its sides at severe angles. Its body expanded and contracted as it took in and released air.

The mosquito tilted its head as it looked at Betsy. Its sucker hung straight down, looking like a vacuum cleaner attachment. Its antennae sprouted from its small head, curled inward on themselves into the shape of a heart.

It had eyes the size of dinner plates, silver-dome eyes. She saw herself reflected in the mosquito's eyes—a nightmare version of herself, a person she did not recognize.

"If you had one wish," the mosquito said, its voice like crawling insects, "what would it be?"

"I would like to help everyone."

"And how would you do that?"

Betsy thought for a moment. "I would like more hands. I have always seen my two hands as helping hands. If I had more hands, I would be able to help everyone in the world. Two hands are not enough to help everyone. I could reach out to everyone in the world. I wish that I had more hands. As many hands as there are people."

She thought of the pile of arms. She thought of how small they had been. She wished she had picked them up, brought them somewhere. She wished she had done something with them, anything other than leaving them there. She thought of Malmoud, his obsidian eyes, the way they radiated anger, the way he touched her ponytail.

"I wish I had been able to bring those children back to life—the way those villagers thought I could. I wish I had picked up those arms and put them back where they belonged, reattached them to their sockets. I wish that I had been able to breathe life into those children's lungs, to give them back the life that was robbed from them."

The mosquito laughed a buzzing laugh. Its heart glowed red inside its body.

The mosquito's face turned into Paul's face. He looked upset. Betsy recognized his voice.

"I'm here with you," he said.

* * *

"I'm here with you at the hospital. You're going to wake up soon and I'm going to be here for you."

Paul sat on a plastic chair next to Betsy's bed. She had a private room. The sky outside the window was overcast. It was going to rain soon. He watched Betsy's eyelids twitch and he thought she must be dreaming.

He did not know how long comas were supposed to last. He thought maybe it was best that she just stay wherever she was.

Paul leaned forward with his elbows on his knees, cupped his hands in front of his mouth, and cried.

She'll need a quadruple amputation, the doctors had said. Symmetric peripheral gangrene. Caused by a malarial infection.

Paul did not know the answers to the doctor's questions about where Betsy had been or what she had done or what she had taken. He only knew what she had told him. She had been to Kenya, to Rwanda, to Sudan. She volunteered with the International Rescue Committee. She had been administering polio vaccinations. It was her dream to help stop polio.

Paul leaned back in his chair and stared out the window. He did not want to think of Betsy spending the rest of her life confined to a bed, without arms, without legs.

He thought that the gray sky was the same sky over Africa. He wondered if these clouds were made of waters that had once been in Africa. It occurred to him that if so, the journey these waters had made was a long and thankless one.

OUT OF STEP IN THE KINGDOM OF OUR LORD

A DAY AFTER HIS thirteenth birthday, Howard Parker received an invitation to join his great-aunt Lillian for Sunday afternoon tea, an invitation Howard received as a welcoming into young adulthood, Howard did, for Sunday afternoon tea was a thoroughly adult activity—according to the rules of the household kept by Lillian—and until that day, significantly, a thoroughly adult activity that had been enjoyed exclusively by Lillian and her dumb, disabled sister Margaret.

That afternoon, the three of them—Howard who had so proudly and so recently been welcomed to young adulthood, his great-aunt Lillian, and her sister Margaret—sat in wicker chairs on the screened-in porch overlooking the old manor's immaculate garden, their whims tended to by the noiseless comings and goings of more than a few inconspicuous helpers, all of whom, it should be said, had been with the family for quite some time. A wide ceiling fan chopped slowly at the humid summer air. Lillian filled Howard's bone-white teacup with particularly fragrant tea, her movements arthritic yet graceful. Margaret sat in her old wheelchair a foot or so back from the table, her rheumy knees buried beneath a thick, plaid blanket. Cataracts clouded her eyes with a swirly, defunct confusion; drool pooled in the corners of her colorless mouth—a stroke the previous summer had rendered her an invalid.

"Howard," Lillian said, saucer held in the flat of her left hand just beneath her chin, teacup pinched between the thumb and index finger of her right hand. "You're becoming a young man and it's time you learned the truth as to why you were put in our charge so many years ago."

The boy studiously set his cup and saucer on the table. Even beneath the lazy chops of the ceiling fan he felt his face flush. The absence of his mother and father had plagued Howard Parker since he could remember feeling plagued by things, things he couldn't otherwise explain, these things. He had often listened enviously to the other boys at his boarding school, far away, out of sight somewhere out there in the mountains, as they bragged of their fathers' professional achievements or recalled fondly—though never too fondly—their doting mothers' comforts.

"Your father died in an asylum—from syphilis," Lillian said, her voice wrapping around that word, Howard imagined, like a massive and unblinking boa twisting around a snowy hare. "Do you know what that is?" He didn't, but before he could say as much Lillian continued. "He contracted it from a prostitute while travelling for business. Your mother…" She took a moment to sharply eye the boy. "Howard, your mother—our niece—was a weak creature whose head was plagued by demons." Here, something spasmed in Margaret's face, something ghastly, locked-in laughter or perhaps a dreadful flicker of daydream. Howard felt as if he might be sick. He stared at his hands in his lap. Lillian ignored her sister, kept her eye sharp, so sharply on the boy. "Sometimes, I fear that you've inherited your disposition from her. Your teachers have complained of an inability to pay attention, that you drift off and do not answer the questions asked of you. Howard, your mother chose eternal damnation when she took her own life. She chose to walk beyond the walls of the kingdom, in the abyss of the damned. It is best that you know—if not only as a precaution—on the off chance that you forget how blessed you are to live in the Lord's kingdom. For this," she swept her arm out, motioning to the garden beyond the railing of the porch, or so Howard thought, "is the kingdom of our Lord."

The significance of Lillian's words, however, were lost upon the boy, whose imagination had gone wild with wondering where, exactly, his mother might be wandering, how far beyond the garden this so-called abyss might be found, and what comforts might lie waiting for him there.

* * *

The blackouts began over the course of the next few weeks, unexpected at first and then, eventually, tolerated, as if the world as Howard understood it were a phonograph record warped from the strains of going round and round—skipping into whole pockets of noise, only to ceaselessly return to music most bewitching. In these moments, these terrible realizations that yet another blackout had come and gone, Howard would simply come to in a place other than the place in which he'd been, often still standing, with no memory of how he'd arrived or what he'd been saying, his hands in such odd formations, like ancient Egyptians painted on stone walls, a gesture half finished, a movement only partially seen through. It alarmed him at first, and then, in a way weirdly inconsistent with his generally fearful temperament, allowed him to feel free, free of being surrounded by, yet never included in, countless conversations with his peers, the words of others simply flowing by unimpeded by his rebuttals, forever unspoken; free of his great-aunt's old and utterly empty house, its endless hallways and drafty drawing rooms and shadowy cooks, maids, butlers, chauffeurs; free of himself—the boy with no parents, plagued, with the father who'd died of complications from something called syphilis, with the mother who'd died in an attempt to escape the torments of—what was the word she'd used?—*demons.* Demons, dear god. That poor soul walking forever in the abyss of the damned, as Lillian had referred to it. It kept him awake at night, it did, all of this thinking.

Most frequently, though, or perhaps it's better said that with eerie regularity, these blackouts hatched Howard out beneath the pale light of the moon, a cold rush of silver sound, whirring, the boy's head spinning with a fevered confusion, discarded in the obsessively ordered and plateaued depths of the manor's garden, chilled to the bone. Other times, he'd come to in what was once his mother's sickroom, or so it was called by a select few members of the staff—and no one else, surely—dust-choked sunlight blaring and impossible to ignore against hastily papered walls, dust chunked in the frills of yellowed doilies, undisturbed forever. In that room, there where he didn't belong, the room in which she'd given in to the whims of her own damned hand, tortured and damned, suddenly struggling to comprehend how much time had escaped him, the boy, Howard, how deep the pocket of noise that had engulfed him, Howard, suddenly overcome, compelled to know what was behind the closet door in this room, the boy pushed open the door in that room, the sickroom, and found the hallway so unlike all the home's other hallways—that dark maw that beckoned him beyond its crooked threshold.

* * *

Here is what the boy learned, what he was able to piece together from his stuttered and clipped conversations with Lillian during their tightly mannered and stifled tea times, as well as the mutterings and overheard musings of the members of the staff, here then is what he learned. He learned that the so-called sickroom was in the process of being converted into an extra bathroom some decades ago, an era in which it remained unknown how many helpers, exactly, were needed to help maintain the manor, to effectively uphold the owner's exacting standards. He learned that the conversion was soon abandoned and forgotten—here, in the narrative he pieced together, Howard occasionally discerned some grumblings about the dangers of a fixed income, the anxieties of dwindling trust accounts, and the frustrations with the expenses of upkeep, the pressure to maintain outward appearance at all costs—and so the so-called sickroom remained abandoned and forgotten, unfinished. He learned that the room was centrally located within the nature-like symmetry of the house's design, like the chambers of a heart within a body, that its unfinished closet was effectively a hole in the heart of the home.

A few tentative yet brave-hearted forays into the room with its giant daybed, its mirrored dresser and end table still cluttered with his mother's things, her perfumer, her brush still tangled with thin strands of near-translucent hair, then through the closet door, and headfirst into the heart-hole's blackness, hovering menacingly within its unfinished walls, an electric lamp to light his way, revealed something of a mirror world, an internal logic to everything Howard understood of his great-aunt Lillian's yawning and magisterial home, such hidden depths, like where the blood goes, squeezed away. An icy wind seemed to rush through its maw every half-minute or so, the breath of a lumbering giant, smelling of the house itself, its very soul, and perhaps, Howard surmised, the cause of the drafts that often made descending from his high bed in the morning a nearly insurmountable task.

The crushing pulse of vertigo, not so dissimilar from the waves of nausea that arose as a result of the blackouts, like a sickening undertow in Howard's stomach, the unwelcome realization that the house contained such depths hidden away, sent him straight to bed with a fever, whirring, always whirring.

When he woke after the most recent blackout and found his strength, when he felt the light of the afternoon sun streaming into his room and falling upon his face and knew it for what it was, the doctor's concerned face coming into focus before him, he learned that weeks—whole weeks—had passed and that he, the boy, Howard, had been discovered in the garden, naked, and feared the worse for wear, as the doctor said, smiling. "Being as that may," the smiling doctor said, "your aunt is very worried about you. She says that you have been ignoring her calls, spending an increasing amount of time alone in the house, unable to be found." And then more talk, more words and bluster, though Howard heard only the doctor's diagnosis: meals to be taken in bed, an hour of walking through the garden during the day, and then rest, more rest, always he should be at rest. In response, Howard nodded, wishing the doctor away, already dreaming of returning to the hallway.

* * *

Other than those regularly scheduled walks in the garden, in the kingdom, during which Howard was accompanied by one of the helpers, always someone different, always someone who seemed to pay him no mind at all, those walks that Howard approached as a regimented activity, walking the same rows in the same order, always, as a matter of precision, perfection, other than those walks he left his bed only at night, Howard did, gliding soundlessly through the halls on bare feet, carefully avoiding the regularly scheduled comings and goings of the helpers as they went about their cleaning, their tidying, and elected only to switch on his electric lamp once he'd safely entered the so-called sickroom, carefully clicking shut the door behind him, there where no one would think to search for him. In addition to his electric lamp, he brought with him, Howard did, a small spiral-bound notebook and the freshly sharpened stub of a pencil, with which he planned to draw a map of his progress in the hopes of not getting lost. Like Theseus, he thought, prepared to slay the Minotaur.

Ten feet or so into the closet and already the warm glow of the sickroom seemed faded, cooling like molten stone as it meets the hiss of tumultuous ocean waves. And then it was like cavernous dimensions unfolded all around him, some sort of gravitational magic act flipped him round and round. The emotion it caused inside him, the boy, was beyond any previous experience. Howard felt particularly bold, emboldened; he switched off the electric lamp and listened intently to the whirring, always the whirring, focused in on the sound of some mysterious machine humming away, burrowed deep within the Earth, or so he imagined.

What purpose could such a machine have, a machine burrowed deep within the Earth? The question plagued him, it did, this question that only hatched other questions.

Set adrift in the darkened corridors of the house, it was not dissimilar from how Howard imagined divers felt, having mistakenly disturbed such quiet beds of silt, their vision suddenly clouded, trapped—a blind panic. It was difficult to discern up from down, left from right; even base notions of direction, of forward and backward, became meaningless, empty language, words without meaning. In those moments, those moments when the onrush of body-feels, the blind panic threatened to send the boy careening into some inescapable abyss, Howard turned on the electric lamp, felt his feet root instantly to the floor once again, earthbound. Then he set to work recording the angles. This was his trick, his method for deciphering the mystery of the moribund house. He wrote down the angles of where the floor met each wall, where each wall, in turn, met the ceiling. He recorded these angles—remembering lessons with the compass in that faraway school, drawing diagrams when needed—recorded them in his notebook, set neatly within neat columns, Howard did, with exacting precision, a scientific acumen, rigorous discipline. Why he did this, why he was doing this, he wasn't quite sure, he didn't quite know. It wasn't as if he had some particular rationale—and so he did not question his instincts, did not allow doubt to sow its seeds. It is important, he said to himself, this work. It is of the utmost importance—to record these angles, to keep a record of these angles. This is work and it is important.

Out went the electric lamp, the numbers and diagrams freshly scratched into his notebook floating through his consciousness like cosmic rails, each one promising some glimmer of truth, to glide the boy closer to something plaguing, something like one of those plagues—and on and on until he woke, once more and forever always, in his bed, sunlight hot upon his skin. And it was there, excitedly, always so excited, he opened his notebook and reviewed the previous night's work, always shocked, strangely pleased, mystified to find that the angles, the diagrams, that they were never the same—as if the hallway was altering itself, folding into itself before breathing back out.

* * *

Bedridden—or so the doctor had commanded—and consumed with obsession, wholly obsessed with the ever-changing hallway, its hollowing existence haunting the boy, plaguing him, Howard Parker suffered through the sunlight-filled days, leaving his room only for the suffocatingly ordered walk through the garden, and awaited each night in a positive fervor. He had filled whole notebooks with the numbers, the angles, his diagrams. He dreamed of numbers, of angles, of diagrams. And when he was awake, he reviewed what he had written: the numbers, the angles, his diagrams. He imagined a code emerging from the data, a message transmitted from deep within the house, from the mirror world, from someone out of step with this reality, or so he imagined, someone who walked beyond the walls that surrounded this, the kingdom of our lord.

And so it eventually came to be that, on one particular Sunday, sun shining, with his health seemingly improving, with the color returning to his cheeks, Howard was permitted to once more join his great-aunt Lillian and her sister Margaret for their regularly scheduled afternoon tea. The boy hoped to use this time to learn more about the house, perhaps its builder, or perhaps whether or not its plans were stored somewhere, under lock and key no doubt, tucked away in some dark office. Upon taking his seat at the table, however, Howard was remiss to see, rather than a cup and saucer set before his great-aunt Lillian, instead the boy was most disappointed to see a single piece of paper, creased in threes and folded outward, bearing the crested insignia of his boarding school, far, so far away.

"Things are going to change," Lillian said. "Things will soon be different. You will see. You will come to understand. You've been out of step with life for far too long, Howard. You've nearly missed enrollment—here, we've only just received notice this week. You'll be held back, Howard. Do you understand the implications of such imperiousness?"

A ship of angelic clouds sailed beyond the sun, opening wide the gates beyond the boy's vision, the gates that led beyond the invisible wall. And in their place, a ray of sunlight like a massive broadsword thrust downward. The sun, this ray of sunlight, it glistened in a strand of Margaret's drool, piercing, a piece of gold glimmering beneath the gurgle of a shallow stream. Somewhere far away, far beyond the mountains, the boy's faraway school. A piece of gold, glimmering. The broadsword blade of an ancient king atop an armored steed, its teeth bared, breath pluming in great clouds upon the steam-wreathed moors, the sun a great black disc burning a cosmic heat, a battlefield of the dead and dying, torn, bloody chunks twisted in clumps of rent and ruined armor, as far as the eye could see.

And then, "I've just asked you a question, Howard." His great-aunt's voice, shrill and tiny in the distance, chopped by the lazy arcs of the ceiling fan. Her voice came closer, louder, and Howard understood that, as he listened to what she said, he understood that she made no attempt to hide her disappointment, her acceptance that he, the boy, was beyond her reach. She understood that he understood and that this was the point. "It is just as I feared," she said, his great-aunt Lillian, but not to him, the boy. No, this she seemingly said to Margaret. "He's more like her, that pitiful creature, than I was willing—or perhaps ready—to admit. The boy is as his mother was. He is forsaken."

Despite the fact that Howard had never once seen Margaret show even the most basic of human emotions, he watched, dumbfounded, as the side of her face unaffected by the stroke slowly contorted into a tight formation of wrinkles that betrayed—and this was unmistakable—what could only be described as smiling malice.

* * *

There would be a car ride, no doubt, and then a train ride, another car ride, this one taking him up a winding mountain road, then through the black gates of the school, so austere, discomfiting, filled with the screeching cruelty of unnamed and countless other young boys, boys like Howard but bigger, stronger, and meaner. His suitcase packed tightly with clothes folded neatly, thumping in the trunk, winding up that winding mountain road. The thin air would make it hard for the boy to catch his breath once the plagues set in, those feelings of being plagued. That first night away, failing to fall asleep on that hard and unforgiving mattress, the blackouts would return, and then the whirring, always the whirring. That weird machine so deep down and far away.

Howard, the boy, he knew that tonight would be his last night in his great-aunt Lillian's house, forever if not for some great amount of time—too much time to lose. He had no time to lose. There was no time to lose. He felt himself, now more than ever, like Theseus, sword raised to the sky and ready to slay the great monster Syphilis, the monster that ate his father and spit out his bones in a pile of perfect angles, a ladder converging with heaven above, always above, occulting behind the lip of the black disc.

* * *

In the garden, awake once more beneath the moonlight, Howard saw how the fauna had swollen to the size of dreadnoughts, the ground littered with black petals, dirt roiling with the black movements of clicking bugs. The flowers opened and closed like leach-lipped mouths. Vines lashed into the sky like the tentacles of a deep-sea monster, sinking to untold depths.

The wheels of her chair squeaked eerily in the eye of the night. Margaret came toward him, one arm—the stroke arm—curled tight against her chest, the other flung loose in her lap. And yet still she came closer. And then she was there, before him, the boy, Howard, holding forth the fetal remains of some puckered flesh sac, its bulbous shape webbed with zig-zagging veins.

Into his hands Howard took the bulb, watching in horror as it unfurled, revealing a small mouth lined with row upon row of flat, dull teeth. Then the sound of laughter, his great-aunt Lillian's laughter, was everywhere, the mouth in his hands pulsating with laughter, as all-encompassing and vivid as a bad dream from which he could not awaken.

* * *

In the darkness of his room that night, his curtains pulled tight before his windows, obscuring his view of the garden below. The angles, the figures, they unfolded their great, dark secret, all on their own. Howard saw them for what they were, a series of clear signals, positives and negatives, ones and negative ones, darkness and light. It was so simple, really. An absurdity. It was the hallway in all its exposed glory, infinite as its pools of black as solid as its walls, its floor, its ceiling.

He wrote down the kaleidoscope of numbers, on and on forever he saw it, uncurling now, and he came to know that this was the answer to all of the hallway's secrets.

He felt it grow again, grow larger but stay the same.

An endless divergence.

In his mind he saw a line hatch from a point in time and space, a snake hatching from its egg, streaking out at an angle to the right before banking back opposite, again and again, each time going out just a bit farther, pushing the walls of the hallway—and subsequently the floor, the ceiling—back beyond, out of sight, into the black beyond.

This, Howard knew, was the blade of the great king's broadsword laid flat across the floorboards, the house twisting itself around its unbreakable steel, forged in the hottest pits of hell, twisting itself into a slow and painful death. A small and menacing snake fell from the empty socket of the king's eye, its tongue a quick flicker of red.

Howard, the boy, he saw himself at the foot of the hallway, standing there a silhouette in a wall of light, and he knew that he also stood at the very tip of this, the hallway's tail. Positives and negatives swirled in his head like planets around the sun, black stars and the brightest, hottest suns, eclipsing one another at perfect intervals, a symmetry of the most flawless machine, humming deep, deep down. He took a step backward, two steps forward—or was that all wrong? Was it not a single step forward and then…

So he began his steps inside forever, free, walking forever outside the kingdom, hand in hand, he imagined, with a woman whose presence he found strangely comforting, as if she were actually several women all at the same time, combined, each one looking after an infinite variation of Howards, all with their own needs, their own emotions, their own fears calling out into the darkness. And although it pained him greatly, he remained unable to look her in the eye, fearful of her monstrous and malformed face, the way he sensed it always changing.

HOUSE OF ABJECTION

WHEN THE FATHER PARKED his long, black sedan at the bottom of the hill, he saw reflected in the rearview mirror the rambling, vine-choked mansion, its hideous and chipped paint bleakly visible beneath the street's lone light. He put his hand on the mother's knee and she immediately stopped her fidgeting beneath the commanding weight of his silver-ringed fingers.

"If you stay in the car, you're going to get cold," the father said to his wife. "We might be in there for half an hour, maybe even an hour, and they're saying that the night is supposed to get quite cold."

The mother sat quiet and still, only slightly turning her head to the side window. Outside, in the early evening dark, the blue and low-hanging leaves of the massive white oak trees shuffled soundlessly. She barely breathed out something like a whispered *no*.

"You can't just sit out here alone and get cold," the daughter said from the back seat. She turned to her husband, the son-in-law, and did something with her face that made him quickly sit forward and say, "She's right, Mother. If you sit out here alone in the car, you're likely to catch cold."

"I won't run the heat for you," the father said. He turned the keys and the car's engine went dumb. "I refuse to leave the keys here in the car. It's not safe for a woman on this side of town—in this neighborhood. This is not a good neighborhood. It's unclean, improper."

The mother breathed a final, limpid protest and removed her husband's hand from her knee. "Okay," she said to no one in particular, "I'll go inside, but I resent being made to feel scared."

It's important to note here that the daughter had been the one to initially suggest a nighttime drive to the mansion.

The four of them had spent the afternoon at the county fair, where the seemingly endless tractor pull had brought down stubborn clouds of all-encompassing blue smoke, swallowing whole the mud-streaked grandstand and dulling the streaked red lights of the carnival rides. The smell of the smoke was sweet and it was everywhere. The old woman calling the bingo numbers in the pavilion at the end of the fairground hacked her way through the penultimate game of blackout. Unsupervised children stalked one another in thuggish groups, playing Jack the Ripper. Although the father's patience with his son-in-law had grown strained toward the end of the day, they'd all gotten along rather well, which wasn't necessarily abnormal.

Originally constructed in the late 1800s, the mansion had first functioned as an inn, serving the laborers of the area's once-booming coal industry. Running a brothel, however, had proved significantly more lucrative, and so the owners, French immigrants, a husband and wife with the surname of Kristeva, had ingratiated themselves with the local peace keepers, offering steep discounts in exchange for their turning a blind eye. By the turn of the century, the mansion was well known as a place of ill-repute. It's said that several unspeakable atrocities were committed within its walls.

No one knows how or why, but eventually the house went vacant; it stayed that way for decades.

Only recently, there was talk of the mansion reopening its doors, this time as a spooky haunted house, a tourist attraction designed for the purpose of entertainment. And so this is how the daughter had come up with her idea. She resented being made to feel like she was missing out on something others were talking excitedly about. "Spooky tours are given throughout the night," she said. "Everyone is talking excitedly about it." The father, who almost always deferred to the wishes of his daughter, said it sounded like fun. The daughter's husband agreed.

Only the mother declined and yet she'd had no real choice in the matter. "Maybe I'll just wait in the car," she said, to which, for the time being, no one had said anything further.

When they arrived at the front door of the mansion, a handwritten sign above the buzzer read, "Press me and wait." The father did as instructed and a shrill bell could be heard from within the house. "I guess we just wait here then," he said. "That's what the sign says to do." The daughter made a face that clearly conveyed impatience and the father shrugged sheepishly in response.

Within a few moments, a metal slot in the center of the door slid open, showing two slightly squinted eyes. "How many in your group?" a woman said in a heavy French accent.

"There're four of us," the daughter's husband said, barely finishing his sentence before the slot slid shut. The door opened and swung wide, revealing a drab, wood-paneled hallway, its lights dimmed and the runner an awful, faded red.

The father motioned for his wife, his daughter, and her husband, to enter before him. When they were all inside, cramped together, the door closed, and there stood the woman who'd spoken to them. She was dressed in black, and though she was obviously quite young her face was heavy with makeup.

Something about the color of the rug reminded the daughter of her menses—more importantly, that she was a few days late. She felt a cramp in her gut; instantly a white-hot line of sweat stippled her upper lip. Although she desperately wished to not be pregnant, she was unable to articulate this to herself. The thought that her cramps were actually an impending bowel movement brought on by the rich foods she'd consumed at the county fair—the elephant ears and pulled pork, fudge sundaes and lemon crushes—slightly calmed her sudden panic. Her skin would react poorly to the sugar, the grease, and this too caused her great concern. She'd have to find a restroom during the tour, she decided.

"Please," said the French woman, "find your way into the drawing room and have a seat. Your host will be with you shortly. He's finishing up a tour of the house with another group at the moment." Then, almost as if it were an afterthought, she said, "My name is Julia." With that she disappeared into the shadows down the hall, the floorboards squeaking softly beneath her steps.

In the drawing room, the father sat alone on a loveseat opposite a television set of some vintage. The daughter and her husband sat together arm in arm on an adjacent—and also quite old—fainting couch. The mother chose to stand in the far corner, her clutch held tightly in both hands.

"How funny," the daughter's husband said, inspecting the fainting couch. "There's a small plaque here that says this very couch belonged to Freud. I'll be." He turned to his wife's father. "You think that could be true, Father?"

"How should I know?" the father said, feigning an intense interest in his wristwatch. He had very little patience for his daughter's husband—the man who'd ripped his little girl from his life—and did his best not to speak to him beyond brief exchanges of necessary information.

The walls of the drawing room were cluttered with bric-a-brac. There were dozens of spooky masks, battered instruments with broken necks, wild and tangled strings, timeworn posters for silent horror films. A nylon rope hung from a light fixture in the center of the ceiling, tied in a noose.

"Lovely," the daughter said, staring at the rope. And then the room suddenly went dark.

The tube television flicked on, flooding the room with silver light. The thick glass screen looped an overscanned black-and-white image of the drawing room, the father sitting on the loveseat, his daughter and her husband on the fainting couch, and the mother, his wife, standing in the corner. The image of the drawing room was suddenly wiped clean of its inhabitants, the grain of the film altered, as the room was devoured by decay. It came on as heavy layers of drifting dust, settling into the crevices of the furniture, forming sloping piles where the walls met the floor.

Abruptly, the screen's harsh light pulled into itself, a small gray dot, and then fell the room into total darkness. It had to have been some clever optical effect, the son-in-law thought, a filter placed over security footage, overexposed images acid burnt and half-eaten by ravenous dust.

And then the television was on again, shedding rapid-fire images one after another: an obese man on the toilet, his genitals hidden by the lip of the bowl; a cat vomiting; gulls pulling flailing and panicked crabs from oceanic whitecaps; an erect and stubby cock, its urethra glistening a compact pearl of pre-seminal fluid; a stallion mounting a mare; the corpse of a rabbit succumbing to decay, swarmed by insects and picked clean, its crumpled and greasy bones piled loose in long blades of grass.

In the corner of the room, near the mother, a lamp buzzed metallic like an alarm clock in a cartoon. The loveseat the father sat on pneumatically lurched forward before hissing back to the floor. All the lights turned on and then off, buzzing. A junked cuckoo clock mounted on the wall hatched a baby-beaked bird, its wired wings flapping.

To everyone's immense relief, the room went dark—and silent—once more. The mother was overcome with the unmistakable feeling that someone had just brushed past her. "Someone just brushed past me," she said, surprised by the eerie calmness of her voice. "There's someone else in the room with us."

A flashlight clicked on in the center of the room, its yellow beam illuminating a face from below, its features freakish and contorted and orangish pink. Although it was somewhat difficult to discern details, the face—seemingly floating there in mid-air—appeared to belong to an elderly man with wild hair. His mouth hung open; his eyes were shut. The room went silent with the collective vacuum of held breath.

The lights turned on—the ghoulish face of the old man filling out and suddenly growing a somewhat hunched, disheveled body, arms and legs and all—and the daughter, once again, clapped her hands. "Amazing," she said. "Where must he have come from?"

"Thank you for choosing to spend your evening with us," the man in the center of the room said, clicking off the flashlight and lowering it, his thick French accent rendering his words near-unintelligible. "My name is Louis-Ferdinand." At this, Louis-Ferdinand did something of a bow, sweeping his hand to his side. "I will be your host for the next hour, personally leading you through our awful home." He giggled.

"They say," Louis-Ferdinand said, scanning the room, leering, "that a man's home is his castle, no? Well, I happen to believe that my home is not only a castle, but a fortified castle. What do I mean by that, you ask? Aren't all castles, by definition, fortified? By that, of course, I mean that the walls of this castle cannot crumble. I exert total control over my domain and everything within it. How is this different from a prison, you ask? And the answer, unfortunately, is that for you tonight this house will be no different from a prison."

Louis-Ferdinand then proceeded to deliver an oral history of the mansion, occasionally pausing for dramatic effect after a particularly horrific anecdote. During this telling, the room would occasionally plunge into darkness. It was a cheap trick, perhaps, but upon being repeated three or four times, its effects became profoundly disturbing to the son-in-law, who grew increasingly conscious of the sound and speed of his breathing, the uncomfortable heat of the blood coursing through his hands, the horrifying idea that anything could be lurking about in that darkness, in all that nothingness. He desperately wished to get on with the tour—and out of this stuffy, cramped room. A wave of nausea brought the acidic sting of bile into his throat when he caught himself thinking that, perhaps, there was nothing beyond the walls of the drawing room—endless and infinite nothingness.

Just as the son-in-law's discomfort became unbearable, the lights came on, seemingly taking Louis-Ferdinand off-guard. "*Quoi?*" A small, hidden door opened in the wall behind the mother and Julia, ducking low through the archway, came quickly into the room, her heavily shadowed eyes wide with fear.

She barked something harsh in French, something that went against the naturally fluid contours of the language, which quickly shushed Louis-Ferdinand. Then, turning to the group, she said, "I am so sorry to interrupt, but I feel the need to let you all know that there is some news in the area. There has been some atrocities. People are dead—perhaps many. It is horrific. These crimes, they occur one town over and I have just heard that the person who committed these crimes—a well-dressed gentleman, according to preliminary reports—has been witnessed stalking around the shadows near this very house."

The father turned to his daughter and said, "Darling, isn't this just fiendishly clever?"

To this, the daughter clapped her hands. "Oh yes," she said. "Brilliant." In an exaggerated voice she said, "Perhaps this maniacal fellow is lost somewhere in this spooky old mansion, just waiting to jump out of the dark and scare us."

Louis-Ferdinand set his flashlight on the mantle behind him. "*S'il vous plait, mes amis*," he said, turning back to face everyone, "this is not part of the tour. *Ce n'est pas* a joke"

"Well of course he's going to say that," the son-in-law said, laughing. "It's all in the name of verisimilitude, isn't that right?" He winked at Louis-Ferdinand.

The Frenchman was visibly repulsed by the son-in-law's attempt at non-verbal communication. He turned and took a few quick strides across the room, standing near the door that led to the hallway. "The chateau is quite old and has many windows," he said, addressing the entire room. "I must ensure that they are all locked, that the castle remains fortified. This place is larger than you could imagine and filled with many *astuces*—unnamable things." With that, he left the room and disappeared into the bowels of the mansion.

Julia lit a cigarette and leaned against the wall. She took a long drag—performing a highly practiced French inhale—and crossed her arms. If she was concerned, her face did not betray it. She seemed to be staring at a memory, through the very walls of the house, staring at something miles away.

Time passed, it's impossible to say exactly how much. The guests, understandably, grew quite restless.

"Listen, Julie—" the father said.

"*Julia*," Julia said, her voice stern. "My name is Julia." She stood up straight, dropped what was left of her cigarette to the floor and crushed it with the heel of her black leather boot.

"Listen, Julia," the father said, seemingly unembarrassed by his faux pas or perhaps oblivious of Julia's scorn, "do you have any idea when your father might be coming back? We've already been waiting for…" He looked down, with great interest, at his wristwatch. "Well, we've been waiting for quite a long time."

Julia laughed. "My father?" she said. "Louis-Ferdinand? No, *vous vous trompez*. Louis-Ferdinand is my lover." She covered her mouth with her curled fingers, a behavior she hadn't entertained since she'd been a young girl in school, hiding her gossipy giggles from her teachers. She pointed a long finger at the father's daughter and her eyes went wide, surprised to be singled out in such a crude manner. "Just like she is your lover, correct?"

The daughter gasped. Her husband noted his wife's reaction out of the corner of his eye, though he kept his face angled toward Julia and did his best not to convey anything other than the kind of boredom that stems from familiarity. The father's face turned blood red, or so thought his daughter, who was once more reminded of her unpunctual menses. When the father spoke, he spoke slowly. "That is my daughter," he said. "And that," he continued, motioning toward his wife, who remained standing near the wall, holding her clutch, also with a carefully studied look of familiar boredom on her face, "is my love—" here he stopped himself short, "that is my wife."

Julia continued to giggle through her fingers. "Ah, of course. How silly of me to get it perversed."

The father, the mother, their daughter and her husband, the son-in-law, watched horrified as Julia attempted, multiple times, to stifle her laughter only to rupture into further fits of something approaching hysteria. "I meant to say *reversed*," she said, between gulps for air. "My language is…not so good sometimes." Tears formed in the corners of her eyes. She waved her hands in front of her face, blurted out a quick, "*Excusez-moi*," and fled through the door and down the dark hallway, in the general direction of her lover Louis-Ferdinand.

"What an awful woman," the son-in-law said.

"Quite rude," the daughter said.

The occasional sound of an old window slamming shut echoed through the long and empty hallways. These echoes drifted apart in time, the distant softness of their sounds correlating directly with their growing infrequency, before stopping altogether. The house buzzed with the raw tension of silence.

The father abruptly took to his feet. "Come on," he announced, apparently addressing the entire room. "This must be some sort of trick—

a test of courage or something. It's part of the tour. If we don't get on with it, we're likely to sit here all night."

"We really should find a restroom," the daughter said.

"Are you not feeling well, my dear?" the mother asked, her voice icy. In response, her daughter merely pouted. She knew better than to solicit sympathy from her mother.

"I think we passed a restroom when we entered the house," the son-in-law said, making his way to the door leading to the hallway. He turned the knob and found that it was locked. "It's locked," he said. He turned to the others. "They've locked us in. Doesn't that violate the fire code?"

The mother pushed in the hidden door Louis-Ferdinand had used to sneak into the room. The door's hinges creaked as the it slowly swung inward, revealing a dark passageway, the horrible noise attracting the reticent stares of her husband, her daughter, and the son-in-law.

"We'll have to go through here," she said, taking time to relish the apparent discomfort of her family.

The father went first, ducking his head to fit through the archway—his wife, her daughter, and the son-in-law followed—and as a group, they moved slowly, one step at a time, the father feeling ahead into the darkness with his hands. Soon enough, a dull light glowed in the distance, evidently showing where the passageway spilled into a concrete room. Hissing and dripping pipes lined the walls, occasionally letting off great charges of steam, their serpentine circuits ornamented with grease-slicked valve wheels and complex meters.

"They sure did do a good job preserving all this old plumbing," the son-in-law said.

"Keep up the pace," the father said. Although he was loath to admit it, he was feeling claustrophobic. His eyes played tricks on him: more than once he thought he saw a glowing red exit sign, only to watch its letters morph into incomprehensible shapes before disappearing altogether. Still, he pushed on, leading the way. His instincts paid off, as they often had throughout the course of his life, because the concrete walls and exposed plumbing eventually gave way to drywall and plywood flooring, the darkness replaced by strings of mining lights hung near the ceiling. The air suddenly became less stuffy. "It's this way," the father said. "I can smell fresh air."

A small ramp led to a flimsy cellar door, the distinctly blue tint of moonlight seeping through the break of its shutters. The father pushed through, half-expecting the door to be padlocked from the outside, only to find that the shutters flipped over effortlessly.

They appeared to be in the courtyard at the center of the mansion. The moon—for it was quite full—illuminated a terribly overgrown and pungently rotting garden, a black gazebo choked with ivy and filled with broken down and rusted machinery. Three floors of windows enclosed the vegetation, much of which appeared Jurassic, overtaking the haphazard stone steps of the walkway, its paths forming something of a circle around a white stone fountain, its large bowl bone dry, the headless statue of a nude woman rising from its center toward the sky, one of her breasts broken away.

Upon setting foot in the courtyard, the four guests split up, each exploring different corners of the garden. The father angled the glass of his wristwatch in the moonlight to make out the hours while the mother judgingly watched him from afar. The daughter inspected the statuary of the fountain while her husband, the son-in-law, was drawn to what appeared to be a long metal cylinder emerging from a wild tangle of broad-leaved plants. Indeed, upon pulling away great amounts of foliage, the son-in-law discovered, to his utmost surprise, that he'd uncovered an almost perfectly preserved battle tank, a Panzer III.

"I'll be," he said. "I guess this is what the Frenchman meant when he was talking about fortification, wouldn't you say, Father?"

The father grunted in response, but he hadn't actually heard his son-in-law's question—in fact, he had mistakenly thought his son-in-law had asked him about *fornication*, which greatly annoyed him, reminding him of that insipid French girl's giggles—for his attentions were fully engaged by the unbelievably strange behaviors of his wristwatch, whose second hand appeared to be spinning backward at a rate he couldn't quite figure out, as if it were irregularly set against the standard, sixty-second minute. For that matter, the minute hand had disappeared altogether, having been replaced with what looked like an earwig pinned in the center of the watch face. The hour hand had turned upward, pointing him accusingly in the face.

Annoyed that the father had once again shirked his attempts at conversation, the son-in-law climbed on top of the tank and opened the hatch. He was tired of being ignored, having spent year after year seeking his affections, made to feel invisible at family functions, like he was nothing. Where he had hoped there would be deep wells of feeling, there was nothing. The word sent a shudder through his body, *nothing.* He wanted to hide. He wanted to be unseen, and so the son-in-law climbed inside the tank and shut the hatch behind him.

Inside the tank, there was only darkness. The son-in-law reached above his head to try to find the hatch but felt only air. He reached out to his sides but felt nothing. For a brief moment, the son-in-law felt as if he were in free fall, his guts queasy with weightlessness—but that couldn't be possible. It wasn't possible. In the blackness, the son-in-law thought he could make out the shape of a door. He made his way to it. It was an ordinary door. He opened it. Through the door there was another door, in the blackness, this one perhaps twice as far away as the first had been. The son-in-law stepped through the door and it disappeared behind him. Or at least he thought he had, but that couldn't be possible. He had no choice but to continue forward. He made his way to the second door and opened it. In the distance he could just barely make out a third door, this one farther than the distance of the first two doors combined. He almost got lost trying to make his way to it, nearly giving in to the temptation to turn around, to try and retrace his steps. Or had he turned around? He couldn't remember. He couldn't see the door in the distance. There was nothing behind him. He didn't know which way *behind* or *in front* was. He was lost in an infinite blackness. He tried to scream but his voice was too small to fill the impossible void that now engulfed him.

"Did you hear that?" the daughter said. "It sounded like a toilet flushing, I think." There was no response. She looked around the courtyard and could see neither her father nor her mother, nor could she see any sign of a restroom. It occurred to her that maybe the sound she'd heard was some sort of a gurgle, perhaps water bubbling up from within the bowl of the fountain, or, and she was unwilling to think about this in any sort of detail, perhaps it was the unmentionable doings of her own digestive system.

In an effort to distract herself from her own bodily functions, the daughter once more focused her attentions on the fountain's statue, thinking how uncanny the resemblance was to her own physique. Of course, the daughter wasn't missing one of her breasts, but that was beside the point. The proportions were almost identical. Double-checking to make sure her mother or father weren't watching her, the daughter quickly undid one of the buttons on her blouse and cupped each of her breasts in her hand, first one and then the other. It did feel as if one was smaller than the other, but that was normal. She repeated the same action, first cupping her right breast and then her left. This time, however, one breast felt significantly smaller than the other.

The daughter stepped into the bowl of the fountain in an effort to more closely inspect the statue. The white stone was badly worn by the weather, discolored in some places, chipped and flaking in others. She thought of her own skin and the stress she'd put it through today—the unhealthy foods, the smoke from the tractor pull—and became intensely fearful that her best days were now behind her. She wished that she could freeze herself in time forever, preserving her beauty for others to admire, and, while contemplating this, unknowingly climbed up onto the stone pedestal with the statue, wrapped her arms around it, and joined it, leaving her unreliable and mortal flesh behind.

At that very moment, it suddenly became clear to the daughter's father that he wasn't looking at his wristwatch at all; in fact, he was looking at a compass, which would go a long way toward explaining the insect-shaped needle straining toward the other side of the courtyard. "We have to go this way," he said, calling to his wife. "The signs are all pointing northward, or southward, whatever."

The wife's husband stumbled his way through the knee-deep vegetation without bothering to check whether his wife followed. He found a door, opened it, ran down a long hallway, nearly tumbled down a steep flight of stone stairs. The insect on his compass was buzzing wildly, its thorax glowing green, its spiracles flexing, telling him he was very nearly there. He made his way down the steps, carefully, one at a time, his hand on the iron railing, the endpoint of his descent lost in a swirling pool of inky shadows.

Now alone in the garden, the woman looked up into the sky and saw a rather sinister thunderhead rolling over the face of the moon. The nighttime air suddenly grew quite cold and she began to shiver. Across the courtyard, she noticed that one of the first-floor windows had been left ajar—Louis-Ferdinand must have missed that one—and so she made her way to it, carefully climbing over its sill, shutting it quietly behind her before locking it in place.

She made her way down a hallway and up a flight of creaking stairs, occasional pulses of blue lightning beaming in through the windows, showing her the way, and then another flight of stairs, yet another, this one spiraling upward into what had to be some sort of tower. In the room's center, a chair set before a small screen.

She sat down. The screen was split into four smaller screens, each intermittently flipping between various nooks and crannies of the mansion—security footage.

Eventually, the small screen in the upper right-hand corner showed what appeared to be a man resembling her husband. She instinctively reached forward and pressed the image with a single finger, enlarging it to fill the screen. Indeed it did appear to be a man who resembled her husband, in what appeared to be a wine cellar, a massive, floor-to-ceiling rack filled with bottles of indeterminate age, the cobble-stone ceiling over his head arched, a few massive wooden barrels on the other side of the room.

The man who resembled her husband seemed to drop something, getting down on his hands and knees and staring at something on the floor. He tracked its movements, whatever it was, across the room and then stood with his back to the camera. Stepping out of the shadows just below the camera's view, creeping up to the man who resembled her husband's turned back, was a tall man wearing an elegant suit and top hat. The woman was unable to see clearly, but he appeared to be holding something before him with both hands. And then, in a flash, the man in the top hat lunged forward, throwing his arms up into the air, a tight string wrapped around each gloved hand. He wrapped the string around the man who resembled her husband's neck and cinched it tight—just as the security footage cut out, the screen blank, showing only the woman's own reflection, surprised, reflected in the light of a particularly intense bout of lighting.

She resented having to think of a grown man being weak, unable to care for himself. She turned to the window at her side, the sprawling view of the town below showing endless rows of other homes, their windows filled with husbands and wives, daughters and husbands, everyone lost and searching for something they would never find.

This was the woman's greatest fear—the wondering. Were they all in on it? Was it all an attempt to make her feel scared? It wouldn't be the first time they'd excluded her from their fun. In fact, her daughter had a lifetime of stealing her husband's attentions, perverting them into her own.

The coldness of the night seeped in through the old window, profoundly discomfiting. The woman looked down to the street far below and saw a long, black car parked beneath the wind-swept leaves of a massive white oak tree. She waited, her heart aching with dread, hoping beyond her wildest dreams that she shouldn't have to see her family get into that car and drive away, leaving her alone and cold and forgotten in this dark tower.

PHANTOMS

ONE DAY THE ADVERTISEMENTS were not there and then the next day they were there and they were everywhere. We heard it said that their presence signaled the beginning of the new economy.

Only two years had passed since they tore down the statue in Firdos Square, since the Americans called to us on loudspeakers—using both Arabic and English—and instructed us to act as if they weren't there, to help make history. The photos of this day soon appeared in the papers and in them we saw a crowd that was much larger than we remembered.

Our memories had betrayed us, we were told.

Like a cloud of smoke, the first of many wide billboards rose above the uneven rooftops of Baghdad, obscuring the trembling rays of the white desert sun. Back alleys that only the day before even brave men wouldn't dare walk down alone were now lined with wheat-paste posters displaying jeans that no one could afford, watches that no one would ever wear, and hairdryers that no one needed. The city's scorched and bullet-flecked pylons were quietly covered with poorly photocopied images of cellphones and cigarettes.

The advertisements were both dull and bursting with color, impossibly at odds with the crushing brown smear of the surrounding desert. There was one for expensive and small containers of honey and there was one for small red cans of cola.

It seemed they were trying to sell the idea of a regular life back to us, in bits and pieces, to those of us who hadn't left yet. And that would have been just fine if we'd cared to know how to go about buying it back, or what do with it once we had it in our possession.

Soon enough a group of young men tore the advertisements down. The Americans stood and watched and held their heavy black guns, bored and youthful and uninterested as always.

Those who have lost limbs say that they still feel what is no longer there. They say that where once there was no feeling there is now a pain whose depth cannot be uttered.

We learned how to wire a grenade and cache it in the wall behind a poster, a mechanism commonly referred to as a victim-operated improvised explosive device. The idea of a victim, of a person, being held responsible for their own death is not unfamiliar to us.

Iraqi Kurds do not typically speak Arabic and most Iraqi Arabs do not typically speak Kurdish. Despite what they might tell you, many of us were taught English at a young age—a language whose usefulness is often preferred by the Kurds to Arabic, by the Arabs to Kurdish. When they first arrived, we'd pass the Americans in the street and jeer and hold up two fingers and say peace and they would look right through us like they couldn't hear us speaking in their own tongue, their eyes scanning the horizon.

Working together, we put up posters that depicted the face of Moqtada al-Sadr looming large over the city's skyline, the silhouettes of brave insurgents beneath him in the foreground, and then we waited for the Americans to do their duty and go about taking them down. Some nights, the muffled pop of a grenade blooms in the distance, an abyss of silence jarred loose within its tremendous echoes.

There is a belief held by some of the men that the desert—the entity that engulfs us all—is a sentient being, a mythical monster that seeks only ruin for the world.

Few forces of nature rival the sheer awesomeness of sand and wind. Sweeping one's doorstep is useless. When your time has come, the sand will find entrance to your home through the smallest of cracks, the thickest of walls. The sand will cast you out to wander its endless yellow seas, where it will then find its way into your shoes, slowing you down, where it will crust your open eyes, occulting all light.

I remember reading a cartoon strip when I was a child, finding the discarded newspaper blowing in the street like so much refuse, taking it home, hiding it away from the others, deciphering its English. Where it came from, I never learned—but there it was, all the same. The cartoon depicted an unclean boy, an American boy, and he referred to his uncleanliness as the dust of ancient civilizations—such an un-American idea.

The dust of our world has hidden us away from the eyes of the Americans. They no longer take us in, see us as human. If they see us at all, they see us as monsters. We are phantoms.

Press a single grain of sand between two fingers with all of your strength and still you will fail to crush it. The harder you press, the more the grain of sand will fortify its strength. A man buried up to his neck in the sand, however, will be pulled in and crushed unmercifully. His death will be slow but his death will be sure.

Talk has begun of ambitious construction projects in the areas surrounding the city—paving the streets, building an elementary school, more billboards—but securing licenses for such endeavors is difficult, despite the opportunity provided by the so-called new economy. The corruption of the local governing bodies is in so many ways like so much dry quicksand: easy to be wary of, impossible to discern.

One of the ancient prophets decreed that genuine men have always dwelt as the lords of the desert, that in the towns dwell well-fed men—draught animals all.

When the safety pin of a grenade is withdrawn, the lever releases and the striker rotates into the primer. When the primer is struck, heat flashes and ignites the fuse. The igniter then sets off the charge. The grenade is filled with what is known as preformed fragmentation, small steel spheres. Spheres are used because cubes take up too much space. These spheres are then released with such force that they rip apart the grenade's cast-iron casing—a storm of biting metal.

The term they so often use to describe this new economy of ours, or so I have seen it said in some of the foreign papers, the way they have so often chose to describe it, with such disdain for the ferocity of carefully chosen words, is to say that this new economy is booming.

A grenade doesn't so much explode as it pops. There is very little smoke, no flame. It is nothing like what you've seen in films. It is the fragmentation, rather than the force of the explosion itself, that is deadly. Of course, if the grenade goes off so close to your body—and this should always be the goal—then the distinction is not necessary.

Nobody tells us where the weapons come from and we do not question their presence. Nobody tells us what to do with them because we already know. When pressed by the Americans for information, nobody knows anything. Nobody has a name. Nobody is scared. There is so much beauty and strength to be found in knowing these things.

Nothing lights up the nighttime sky quite like the spectacle of tracer fire as it arcs over the rooftops. I imagine it to be not dissimilar from the way the starry corpse of the universe will appear as it pulls itself apart, light stringing into spaghetti strands, a hungry black hole swallowing all of creation.

All throughout the city streets, the dogs bark. Animals know something that we do not. Animals know a hunger that we do not. They sense something that we believe to not be there at all. The dogs know. The noise of their pain is a dream whose clutches cannot be escaped.

THE FINAL DIAGNOSIS OF DOCTOR LAZARE

AT FIRST THERE WAS nothing, and only in his awareness of this nothingness did something emerge. There were two identical rooms—two sets of four white-tiled walls gleaming with light—suspended over a black void. He saw them as if from above, these two identical rooms, miniature glass cubes, and within each room he saw a bed and a chair facing the bed. He felt himself drifting toward the two rooms, worried at first that he might slip into the depthless space between them, becoming lost forever in the black void. Yet as he drew closer, still caught in the drift, the two rooms pulled together and became one, sharing the same light.

He felt the warmth of the light on the backs of his hands and upon his face. Air filled his lungs. He opened his eyes.

The man lay in a twin-sized bed tucked tight beneath white sheets. Sunlight filled a wire-reinforced glass window. Nearby an empty wooden chair faced him. The walls of the room were white tile, gleaming and sanitized. He heard a sound like the rattle of an alarm and saw a steam radiator in the corner where before there had been nothing.

A doorway appeared and a man wearing a white lab coat and expensive pants walked through it. He sat in the wooden chair opposite the bed, crossed one leg over the other, and laid his clipboard against his thigh. Then he removed a retractable pen from the breast pocket of his lab coat, clicked it, and offered a sterile smile.

"Good morning," he said. "I am Doctor Lazare."

"Where am I?" the man in bed asked, surprised by the sound of his own voice, the way it rattled around inside his head, so tinny and alien. He cleared his throat.

"You're here with us," the doctor said, scribbling notes as he spoke. He paused a moment, then met the man's eyes. "Before we continue, I need you to promise me that we won't have any more violent outbursts—not like yesterday." He smiled again. "Can you promise me that?"

"Yesterday?"

"You don't remember." The doctor seemed to consider this for a moment, then uncrossed his legs and stood. He wheeled close a metal table—which somehow the man had not previously noticed—and used the controls on the side of the bed to raise the man into a sitting position. Finally he removed a ruled notepad and a yellow pencil from the side pocket of his lab coat and placed them on the table.

"I'd like to administer a test," the doctor said. "Don't worry—there are no right or wrong answers. It's merely a method of measuring the progress of your recovery."

"My recovery?"

"Your recovery," the doctor repeated. He removed a sheet of paper from his clipboard and laid it on the table beside the notepad and the pencil. The paper contained four diagrams drawn with black lines. "Please take a moment to familiarize yourself with these diagrams. After a few moments, I will ask you to re-create them."

The man studied the diagrams. The first diagram showed a single square, and then below that a set of four equal-sized squares, and then below that a set of nine equal-sized squares. The second diagram showed four sets of two overlapping circles. The interior of each circle was shaded differently, as were the overlapping regions. The third diagram showed yet another circle. From that first circle two arrows pointed to two additional circles. From each of those second two circles, two arrows pointed to two additional circles, resulting in a total of seven circles. And the fourth diagram was a simple octagon, which resembled a stop sign.

Doctor Lazare took away the sheet of paper that contained the diagrams. "Now," he said, "please re-create what you saw using the pencil and the notepad. I'll leave you alone to concentrate. When I return, we will review your work and discuss the results." He crossed the room and quietly closed the door behind him.

The only sound in the room was the radiator rattling, which the man did his best to ignore. In doing so, the sound disappeared. He made to reach for the pencil and saw that his right arm had been handcuffed to the bed rail. The handcuffs were connected by a silver-link chain, which afforded him extra range of motion, just enough to reach the pencil on the table.

He looked to his other arm and saw that it was wrapped in pressure bandages. When he attempted to move the fingers on his left hand, he found that they did not respond. A plastic oxygen sensor was clamped over the tip of his left index finger. He traced the plastic tube from the sensor to a monitor on an extendable rolling pole. The monitor beeped at a regular rhythm, and a small green light on its face held constant.

All of these things he accepted as truths, facts beyond manipulation.

The man picked up the pencil in his good hand and started to re-create the diagrams as he remembered them. When he was done, he set the pencil down on the table next to the notepad and looked over his work. With his mind free, the sound of the radiator returned.

Dr. Lazare came back into the room. This time he did not sit in the chair but rather stood next to the bed, looming. "Let's see how you did," the doctor said, once more laying the sheet that contained the diagrams on the table next to the notepad.

The man looked at the diagrams on the paper and then looked at what he had drawn on the notepad. He looked back and forth from one to the other several times.

"But these aren't the same diagrams you asked me to re-create," the man said, angling his line of sight upward to better see the doctor's face, which now appeared distorted, disproportionate somehow. "You've switched out the first piece of paper with another."

"I'm afraid that's not true," the doctor said. The expression on his face was difficult to make out. He crossed his arms over the clipboard, holding it close against his chest.

"You've tricked me," the man said, looking back to the diagrams, tapping his finger against the doctor's paper. "These aren't the same."

"Most peculiar," the doctor said. He scratched a few notes on his clipboard. "There's nothing to worry about. You're merely exhibiting the symptoms of your illness."

"My illness?"

"Your illness," the doctor repeated. "I know that your recovery has been difficult for you, but I assure you that we are making progress. I'd like you to continue reading from the diagnostic manual." He gestured to a thick hardcover book on the end table beside the man's bed, both of which the man had failed to notice earlier. "Take notes on anything that takes your attention, anything at all, and we will discuss your notes during our next meeting."

After the doctor left, the man lay in his bed and continued listening to the radiator rattle, the steady beeping of the monitor, the beating of his heart. He tried to move the fingers on his left hand. He wondered what kind of illness he had, whether or not it was serious, how long he had been here, and who had brought him here. He wondered when he might leave, where he might go. He wondered who he was—and in this he felt eerily adrift.

Eventually he picked up the book on the end table. It was quite heavy, and difficult to manage with only one hand. The book was titled *A Diagnostic Manual of Illnesses* and its author was Doctor Lazare. He saw a dog-eared bookmark tucked within its pages. The man opened the book to where he could only assume he'd previously left off and began to read.

* * *

Without recovery the severity of the patient's suffering is likely to increase until it becomes unbearable. A patient with an illness whose suffering becomes unbearable will find relief only in death. Only the recovery process can prevent the death of the patient.

The patient suffering an illness cannot begin the recovery process without first understanding the "root" of the illness. When referring to the root of the illness we refer not only to the "cause" of the illness, but also its Thanatotic drive (see Appendix II for more on the various drives). Identifying the cause of an illness is helpful in classifying its symptoms; it is true. In isolating the pure function of its Thanatotic drive, however, we are able to best understand the behaviors of the illness, and only in understanding those behaviors—or "behavioral inhibitors"—can we begin to address and correct them, thus relieving the suffering of the patient.

The root of the illness must first be pinpointed through a process of elimination. By writing down the symptoms of the illness, and subsequently discussing these symptoms with a licensed medical professional, the patient can then consult the diagnostic constellation chart found in Chapter 18. The diagnostic constellation chart offers a visual representation of the shared symptoms of all catalogued illnesses, i.e., those illnesses officially diagnosed by licensed medical professionals. Once a list of the symptoms of the illness has been compiled, and subsequently cross-referenced against the diagnostic constellation chart, the patient can then eliminate inapplicable behavioral inhibitors. Upon completion of the elimination of inapplicable behavioral inhibitors the patient can begin the recovery process, which can prove long and painful, fraught with frequent pitfalls. Therefore it is of the utmost importance that the patient learns to rely solely on the guidance of his doctor.

***

Later that day, or perhaps even early the next day, an orderly dressed all in white—white shoes, white pants, white shirt—entered the man's room. His head was shaved and gleaming. Using a small key attached to a ring full of other keys the orderly unlocked the man's handcuffs, removed them from the bed rail, and then slid them around the armrest of a nearby wheelchair, tightening the single strand with a metallic ratcheting sound.

After the orderly helped the man out of his bed and into the wheelchair, he reattached the plastic sensor to the end of the man's left index finger. "You have a visitor, lucky duck," the orderly said, rolling the monitor with one hand, and guiding the chair with the other. "She's waiting for you in the courtyard."

The orderly's white shoes were silent on the tile floor, the movement of the chair smooth—everything in motion. Caged lightbulbs hung from the arched hallway ceiling, passing in a procession. They entered a large room where a television set blared empty, indiscernible noise. A few people in plain white clothes, robes, and paper gowns milled about aimlessly. Everyone's heads were shaved and gleaming. Then the shrill sound of an electric buzzer hung stubborn in the air, a set of double doors opened as they approached, and a rush of daylight overwhelmed the man's senses.

He shielded his eyes with his good hand and saw the light through the webbed skin of his fingers. Everywhere still he heard the sound of the electric buzzer. He closed his eyes and saw black spots, negative impressions of the sun, drifting.

His chair came to a sudden halt and the man felt the orderly set the footbrakes. He opened his eyes. The sky was limitless, the air clean. In the distance he saw a mountain range, chunks of dark stone dusted white. The rest of the scene soon fell into place: a placid black-water pond, stone walkways, wide lawns. He saw women and children dressed in their finest clothes. He saw couples walking hand in hand, sitting on benches, feeding ducks in the pond. He heard the sounds of laughter, murmurs of distant conversation.

"Malcolm?" It was a woman's voice, echoing as if through a long tunnel. He heard it again, more insistent this time. "Malcolm, can you hear me?"

There she was, sitting on a park bench beneath the partial shade of an old tree. She wore a wide-brimmed hat and an overcoat. She wore stylish, oversized sunglasses. Her hands were folded in her lap and the sharp lines of her diamond ring caught the light of the sun.

"Are you talking to me?" the man asked, turning to look over his shoulder, as if she might be talking to someone behind him. No one else was nearby; apparently the orderly had elected to give them privacy, sneaking away soundlessly. The monitor softly beeped.

He turned to the woman and saw her face change in a manner he couldn't quite understand. "Of course I am," she said. "Who else would I be talking to?" She paused, expectant. "Malcolm, please, we've come all this way."

"We?" Next to the woman sat two boys in school uniforms, identical twins. They had the same tousled blond hair, the same blue eyes, the same small noses and ruddy cheeks.

These sudden intrusions of things and people he hadn't previously noticed were surely a symptom of his illness, he thought. He would have to remember to write that down.

"Hello, Dad," the boys said in unison.

Malcolm stared at the two boys in silence.

"Darling," the woman said, "don't be rude. Say something to your sons."

"My sons," Malcolm repeated. The two boys looked at him, expectant, waiting for their father to speak to them as fathers speak to their sons. He didn't know what fathers said to their sons, so he decided to tell them what he did know. Perhaps, he thought, it would mean more to them than it did to him. "My name is Malcolm. I have an illness. I'm working on my recovery."

Malcolm was unable to discern whether the boys were bored or terrified, the way they looked at one another wide eyed. He searched the eyes of the boy closest to him, looking for a clue. He saw that the boy's eyes resembled two glass cubes. Looking deeper he saw that within each of those two cubes stood a bed and a chair facing the bed. He settled back into his wheelchair, thinking about what this might mean. Then he took out the notepad and with his good hand wrote down all of the things that took his attention, just as the doctor had instructed.

A few moments passed, during which no one spoke. When he finished writing, Malcolm looked around the courtyard. Two of the ducks rose from the black waters of the pond as if levitating, motionless, and then darted off into the sky. He watched the ducks shrink down to the size of black dots, and when he blinked they disappeared.

They had escaped, he thought. They must be the lucky ones.

"Darling," the woman said, her voice thin, nervous, pulling him back from his drifting thoughts. "Have your doctors said anything about your release?"

"My release?"

"When you'll be allowed to return home."

"Return home," Malcolm repeated. He folded and unfolded these words in his mind, repeating their sound until they seemed to lose their meaning. "How long have I been away from home?"

The woman ever so slightly shook her head. "Darling, I don't..." Her lips were pressed tight together, a crooked white line, and her chin appeared pitted, quaking. "I don't understand." She started to sob.

"How long have I been away from home?" he said again, insistent this time.

Nobody answered him. The woman continued to sob quietly. The two boys had turned away, looking in opposite directions. One rested his chin on his closed fist; the other slouched with arms crossed over his chest. He saw now that they weren't twins at all, brothers perhaps, but certainly not twins. One of the boys was clearly older than the other, his facial features more pronounced. One of the boys had hair that was darker than the other's.

Malcolm wrote in his notepad that two things that initially appeared to be the same will sometimes reveal themselves to be different. He wrote that he should not be fooled by deceptive appearances. He tapped the rubber pencil eraser against his lower lip, thinking. Then he continued. If two cubes appear in place of a person's eyes, then the black void must be the space inside that person's head. He remembered what it felt like to drift above the black void, the fear of the gulf between two things, where there was nothing at all. And if there was a place where there was nothing at all, then surely no person could exist there.

"I don't believe that you're real," he said calmly to the woman. He looked at the two boys. "All of you. None of you exist."

From behind her dark glasses, tears slipped down the woman's face. She didn't say anything as she stood and approached the two boys, gently touching each one on the shoulder, guiding them down the stone walkway until they had disappeared like ducks in the sky.

The monitor beeped, signaling that everything was normal and that nothing had changed.

* * *

The patient's illness will ultimately define the patient's reality. "Symptoms," by definition, are subjective evidence of the illness itself. Additionally, these symptoms may indicate the existence of something hidden, such as a previously undiagnosed illness, or a trauma buried in the unconscious. Just as the body serves as a representation of the goings-on within, that-which-is-real occurs in a "submerged" reality beyond the surface level. Therefore, the reality of the patient can never be fully understood by the patient. This circulus in probando *is known as the "dilemma of rings." After all, what is a circle if not a line that has lost its way, doomed to repeat the same course of action again and again?*

As previously noted, conducting an investigation into the illness at its root can occur only after the symptoms of the illness have been catalogued and cross-referenced against the diagnostic constellation chart. With this process completed, and with the recovery process underway, the patient—working under the supervision and guidance of the licensed medical professional—can peel back the surface of reality and reveal that which is hidden: the "event" of the illness. The event of the illness is the underlying cause in its primary state. Such an event can only be witnessed under the skin, so to speak. By peeling back the patient's skin, the subjective nature of the illness will be revealed as an objective reality, where it can then be studied and better understood.

The dilemma of rings states that nothing can be proven to be real unless it has been correlated with some other person, place, or thing already present in reality. Some of the most difficult-to-diagnose illnesses are "nested" in this very idea. The danger here, of course, is that the patient should lose their way during the diagnostic process, therefore losing their grip on reality, as well as the thoughts and memories from which their identity is constructed.

* * *

From then on Malcolm spent his mornings in bed reading, his afternoons watching television in the common area, his evenings back in bed correlating his symptoms. He worried that he wasn't making sufficient progress in his recovery. All of the notes he wrote, the handfuls of unmarked white pills he swallowed, the time he spent reading, cross-referencing against the diagnostic constellation chart—and still his recovery seemed as elusive as ever. He worried that he had lost his way. He worried that he was turning in circles.

Then one day the orderly used the key attached to the ring full of other keys to unlock Malcolm's handcuffs, removing them from the bed frame. He then fastened the strand around the monitor's rolling rack. "The doctor would like to see you now," he said.

When he arrived at the doctor's office, Malcolm asked about the purpose of the monitor, and why he must remain attached to it.

"It assures us that everything is all right," the doctor explained from behind his wide desk. "That beeping noise you hear every so often? Well, that tells us that your vital signs—your heartbeat, breathing rate, temperature, and blood pressure—are as they should be. The signal is monitored from a control room. At any given moment on any given day, each and every patient here with us is accounted for. We must ensure that everything is in its right place, so to speak."

"In its right place," Malcolm repeated. He folded and unfolded these words. Was everything in its right place? Or was everything—objects, people, shadows—placed in such a way so they only appeared to be in their right place?

He took note of the things found within the doctor's office, in case something might appear to be out of place, in case he had missed a clue. There was a full-body model of a skeleton propped up in the corner. Various academic degrees in glass frames had been carefully arranged on one wall. On another wall, a laminated poster that explained first aid for cuts and scrapes. Although he wasn't quite sure why, Malcolm decided that this second poster was meaningful.

"What else is taking your attention?" the doctor asked.

Malcolm explained his concern that he was turning in circles.

"It's your paranoia," the doctor said, writing all of this down. "Perhaps it's worsening as a result of the anxiety you feel regarding the speed of your recovery."

"Yes," Malcolm said. "It's worsening—the anxiety."

"But that's wonderful news," the doctor said, smiling. "Not that you have anxiety, no. But rather the fact that we've now identified and diagnosed your paranoia signifies that your recovery is on track. After all, acute paranoia is one of your symptoms. Remember?" He gestured to Malcolm's notepad. "See for yourself."

Malcolm opened his notepad and thumbed through the pages until he found what he was looking for. There, in the middle of a page full of other symptoms, he saw the words "I am paranoid."

"Did you write this in here?" Malcolm said, turning the notepad so the doctor could see.

"No," the doctor said. "But that you think I did is a good sign. Your accusation correlates your emotions with a thing outside of yourself."

Malcolm watched the doctor's face closely.

"My advice for you," the doctor said, "is to change up your routine. You've become too set in your ways and it is interfering with your discovery process. Get outside your comfort zone. Do something unexpected."

The next night, still handcuffed to the beeping monitor, Malcolm decided to heed Doctor Lazare's advice and explore the halls beyond his room—to change up his routine. He went wherever his attention guided him. He rode an elevator down to the basement, passed by signs that said

Do Not Enter. He went down a hallway lit with dim, flickering light, where puddles of rust-colored water had formed on the floor.

Exposed plumbing snaked along the ceiling, steam coursed loudly through the pipes, and industrial machines pounded away in unseen rooms. Eventually Malcolm found a metal door with a placard that said *Control Room.* He tried the door handle, expecting it to be locked, and was surprised when it opened all on its own. The room was dark; the only source of light was a work lamp lying on its side on the floor, as if it had been swept off the nearby desk. An audio monitor hidden somewhere in the shadows warbled a stream of static in which he discerned faint weeping sounds.

"Hello?" he said. "Is anyone here?"

Malcolm shut the door and locked it—in case anyone might be following him. Then he carefully made his way to the overturned lamp, picked it up, and put it back on the desk. Angling the light, he saw a large bank of television monitors, all of which had been turned off, the dozen or so screens smooth as black stone. Countless sheets of loose-leaf paper, each one covered with sequences of numbers and codes, were strewn about the floor.

A crack of light was visible on the far wall—an open door leading to yet another room. This second door had a sign on it that said *Danger: Power Supply.* He pushed through.

The pounding of the industrial machines grew louder. Malcolm found himself standing at the foot of a long hallway. A florescent light hung flickering from the ceiling, suspended by a coil of thick wire. More exposed plumbing—the twisting tubes and pipes like so many veins exposed beneath stripped-away skin—covered one wall. Opposite the steam pipes he saw a wooden desk and an empty chair, not dissimilar from the one in his room, the same wooden chair he had seen reflected in the eyes of his son.

The end of the hallway was obscured by shadow. He felt drawn to the darkness. His heart pounded in rhythm with the unseen machines. He remembered what it felt like to drift above the black void, freed of the weight of his flesh, these handcuffs, his illness.

Malcolm's progress was halted by a rusted fence that spanned the width of the hallway. He laced the fingers of his good hand through the cold chain link. There was no going past this point; there was no gate, no entranceway, no way to get through. And besides, beyond this fence he saw only darkness, endless hallway. He turned around.

He saw the body from some distance—wearing the unmistakable uniform of a security guard—slumped forward in the wooden chair behind the desk. The handle of a surgical scalpel protruded from the smile-shaped wound in the body's abdomen. Malcolm maneuvered around the darkly shimmering puddle of blood on the floor, careful not to get any on his white shoes, the wheels of his monitor's rolling rack. Then he leaned forward to get a better look at the guard's face, which was turned sideways in the low light, resting flat on the desk. It was a mess beyond recognition. A series of deep cuts dragged along the jawline, across the hairline, and around the eye sockets. His lips had been mutilated; one of the eyeballs had burst.

Malcolm slid free the scalpel and put it in his pocket; it might yet prove useful.

He closed the door to the dark hallway behind him, muffling the sound of the industrial machines, and returned to the familiar light of the hallway. From there he easily found his way back, as if led by an invisible hand.

* * *

The primary danger of self-diagnosis stems from a lack of objectivity. If the patient self-diagnoses as nyctophobic, for instance, they will then justify any decision made to avoid darkness as a means of not worsening their illness. Yet an avoidance of this nature does not aid recovery. Perhaps the event of the illness occurred under the cover of night? Such an event, allowed to lie dormant, protected by the patient's self-diagnosis, shall remain occulted. And if these occultations are not interrogated rigorously, the recovery process will be impeded.

The very nature of the recovery process—frequently painful, discomfiting—is likely to result in self-diagnoses that "insulate" the patient from identifying the most insidious symptoms of their illness. Here it is the responsibility of the licensed medical professional to guide the patient to confront the bias of their self-diagnosis. A patient who lacks the guidance of a licensed medical professional is statistically far more likely to experience a variety of mental breaks, including dissociative amnesia, dissociative identity disorder, or delirium.

Patients near the end of the recovery process are most at risk of a biased self-diagnosis. Despite the recovery of the patient being of utmost importance, as previously stated, the patient on the verge of full recovery will seek to remain within the "embrace" of the illness, rather than experience the unknown. It is a truly dangerous time, and one in which the patient could potentially lose touch with "knowable identifiers"—or the very objects that tether the subjective nature of the illness to objective reality. Identifiers such as feelings, thoughts, memories, and impulses can become "estranged," resulting in acts of violence motivated primarily by the illness.

***

Malcolm sat on a paper-covered medical exam table, his slipper-covered feet resting on the retractable step. The room was small, brightly lit. Several glass jars lined the counter along the wall, each containing an unrecognizable mass of flesh suspended in green-tinged liquid. The steel sink was spattered with dried blood, and the walls were littered with laminated posters that detailed first aid for cuts and scrapes—identical to the poster in Doctor Lazare's office.

A woman wearing a white lab coat entered the room. "Good afternoon," she said, heading straight for the sink. "Are you ready to have your bandages removed?"

The doctor washed her slender hands, seemingly undisturbed by the bloodstains in the sink. When she was finished, she retrieved a pair of scissors with a ribbon handle from one of the cupboards. She asked Malcolm to extend his arm with his palm facing the ceiling. He tried to look her in her eyes—to get a glimpse of her hidden self—but she did not meet his gaze, remaining entirely focused on the task at hand.

"Seeing a newly healed wound for the first time can be quite unpleasant," she said. "Please be prepared for unwelcome thoughts."

Cradling Malcom's hand in hers, she snipped through the bandages from his wrist to his elbow. The severed strips fell away, revealing a network of jagged incisions neatly stitched together with dark thread. With his good hand Malcolm traced the scabrous tissue with the tips of his fingers. He felt nothing.

"Now we need to remove your stitches," the doctor said. "You may feel some slight discomfort."

Using tweezers, she gently plucked at the thread, sliding the sutures up and out of the skin, and snipped each knot with the scissors. When she was finished, she cleaned the wounds with a cotton ball soaked in cool rubbing alcohol.

"All done," she said. "Can you wiggle your fingers for me?"

Malcolm tried to do as she asked but his fingers did not respond.

"Close your eyes," the doctor said. "I'm going to touch the tip of each finger in no particular order. Please tell me if you feel anything." She paused. "What about now?"

"No."

"And now?"

"Nothing."

Malcolm opened his eyes, felt the world spin away from all he had known. The posters on the walls were gone and the walls themselves had been replaced by unadorned concrete. A small, barred window near the ceiling let in slanting beams of cold blue light.

He turned once more to the glass jars, seeing now that the smallest contained a pair of eyeballs, the next largest held what appeared to be a severed hand, and the largest contained a human heart.

Malcolm studied the doctor. "Who are you?" he said. "Where am I?"

Ignoring his questions, the doctor pried open Malcolm's eyelid with her thumb and forefinger, shined a small flashlight into one eye, then the other—blinding him. When the light clicked off, Malcolm saw black suns drifting. The black suns dragged darkness over the walls, and the darkness was like an infection spreading through the room. A jagged fissure ripped through the concrete wall, a cracking noise as loud as thunder, beginning near the floor, and then extending like the branches of a tree.

He tried to stand, to flee the expanding dark, but he was stuck in place. He was strapped to an emergency restraint chair. The straps bit into his shoulders, his forehead; another strap spanned his lap. His wrists were strapped to the armrests, his ankles to the chair legs.

"Tell me," the doctor said, "what do you think happened to your arm?"

He recalled only the black void. "I don't know."

"Think, Malcolm."

He felt himself drifting once more, weightless. "I can't."

"For the sake of your recovery," she said, raising her voice, "it's important that you remember. Can you recall anything about the day before you woke up handcuffed to your bed?"

He closed his eyes and let the black void swallow everything outside himself, joining with the spreading infection of the room, the drifting black suns ringed with light.

A single still image took his attention, unfinished and dark around the edges, like a great room lit by crooked fingers of lightning. He saw himself sitting behind Doctor Lazare's wide desk, in the room with the model skeleton propped up in the corner, its hollow eyes gaping.

More images followed, only these were not merely still, but moving—vivid with sound and color. He saw wide-eyed patients dressed in white disappearing behind locked doors, dragged kicking and screaming through the tunnels deep beneath the building. He saw men and women strapped to gurneys wheeled down darkened hallways. He saw bone saws and large-gauge needles held up under blinding lights, the mouth of a furnace lit up like an inferno. And then he saw a security guard roaming the empty halls, making his rounds, stopping at each door, each individual cell, to peer through the viewing pane.

Malcolm took in all of these sights and more as he watched the wall of closed-circuit TVs in the control room. He wore a white lab coat and expensive pants. He twirled a retractable pen in one hand, nervously clicking its button. On one of the screens he saw the security guard descending the steps into the basement, sweeping the beam of his flashlight across the hall. In a fit of rage Malcolm swept the items on the desk onto the floor—the reams of paper that contained readouts of each patient's vitals, the small radio that piped in sound from the nearby operating theater—and the light of the work lamp angled toward the ceiling. He turned off the TVs, plunging the room into darkness.

He stalked through the shadows, coming up behind the security guard and plunging the scalpel into his side. He watched himself slashing frantically at the security guard's hands and fingers as he attempted to protect himself. And then he was back in his room, in his office, pacing back and forth, his hands pressed to the sides of his head.

Another flash of lightning lit up his office an electric blue. The life he had built for himself, the knowledge he had accrued, the accomplishments and laurels that stacked like cadavers—all of it would soon be gone. He'd gotten careless.

There was only one thing left to do. He sat down, opened a drawer in his desk, and removed yet another surgical scalpel. Then he took off his lab coat, rolled up his sleeve, laid his arm flat on the surface of his desk, and with his good hand—his operating hand—pressed the cold blade against his flesh.

He held his hand against the wound, tried to hold it all in, but it forced its way through the spaces between his fingers, escaping him. He felt dizzy, his vision fading, lights drifting. Always he felt like he was drifting.

Malcolm opened his eyes. The doctor stood before him, watching him, taking notes.

"Tell me, Malcolm," she said. "Tell me what happened. Tell me what you saw."

The whole room trembled, as if it might collapse. He tried to read the doctor's face, to get a sense of what she was thinking, but her features had gone smooth, a single continuous surface. She could be anybody at all. And if that were true, then nobody was anybody.

"I can't be who I think am," he said. "It's just a symptom of my illness."

The cracks in the wall ripped open. Great slabs of black stone crushed the light out of the room. In the newly hatched darkness Malcolm drifted, rushing toward the limitless black beyond. Wind whipped at his face, the rush of sound all consuming. He opened his eyes.

* * *

If the state or quality of the patient's reality is fractured—if the subjective reality is wholly isolated from an objective context—then, with no other recourse, the patient will unerringly search out that which best "mirrors" what is real. The patient does this unknowingly, seeking only to maintain some semblance of the status quo, a reflection or echo of the safe and the known. Anything beyond the known, in the patient's limited perception, will constitute a continuation of the illness, and result in further suffering.

In cases of extreme fracturing, the patient may become fixated on the fracture lines themselves, rather than the so-called pieces of reality. To illustrate this point, imagine the patient staring into a broken silver-glass mirror, and believing that the material behind the reflective surface is their reflection. Such fixation is likely to result in a total loss of the thoughts, memories, and feelings that constitute the "self" (further elaborated upon in the diagnostic constellation as "identity delusion disorder"). This disorder is typically the result of violent trauma spurred by an accumulation of paranoia. Essentially, the patient who believes that they are being invasively investigated or pursued by unknown or faceless entities will lash out at any real or imagined investigators or pursuers, and in doing so likely commit heinous crimes.

Malcolm, if you're reading this, if you've made it this far, then surely you realize these words are intended to release you from the grip of your illness, to relieve you of your suffering. Surely you realize that these words were written only for you—by you. You're in the final stages of your recovery. As such you must be careful when making your diagnosis. Think of all the evidence. Remember what it means to be a person with a name and a family, with memories and feelings, and the freedom to live a life of your own choosing. Do not give in.

* * *

The man who was Malcolm stood in the center of the room and turned in a circle. When he came to a stop, he saw a bed and a chair facing the bed—just like before. Still he was unsure if this was his room or if it was merely meant to resemble his room.

Things emerged from nothingness all on their own, he saw that now. He saw a steam radiator in the corner, a wheelchair beside the bed, and the diagnostic manual lying page-down on the floor, its cracked spine displaying the name of its author: Doctor Malcolm Lazare. He saw his monitor on its rolling rack, its constant green light, the silver gleam of the handcuffs, the plastic sensor clipped to the end of his finger. He searched out anything that was not in its right place, and one thing took his attention immediately. Where once there had been a wire-reinforced window there was now a full-length mirror.

He studied his reflection in the mirror: a faceless man in a white hospital gown. He remembered something he had once written down. *Two things that initially appear to be the same sometimes reveal themselves as different.* Thus, it stood to reason that two things that appear to be different can reveal themselves to be one and the same.

There was nothing—he was nowhere, drifting—and only in his awareness of this nothingness did something emerge. Where he should have seen the man who was Malcolm, he instead saw a body with its secrets exposed to the world, a skeleton poorly disguised in a suit of skin. His skin hid who he really was. It was his skin that buried the root of his illness. He must emerge from beneath the deceptive surface once and for all.

Malcolm pressed the blade of the scalpel against his forehead, just below his hairline, felt the cool metal come up against bone. There was no pain. He pulled a line down the outer edge of his face, the blade gliding cleanly along his ear, below his chin. He made an identical incision on the other side of his face. Then he traced a circle around one eye, the other eye, drawing so much blood he could no longer see.

He worked without aid of sight, snuck his fingers deep beneath the lip of skin at the top of his forehead and began to slowly peel away the featureless mask, the deceptive thing that hid his true self. The sticking skin was stubborn, his fingers slipping, but he remained intent. He prepared himself for unwelcome thoughts.

There was blood everywhere. His hospital gown was completely soaked through, clinging to every contour of his body like a second skin. A sudden shudder of dizziness sapped the strength from his legs, his knees gone rubbery. The monitor released a frantic high-pitched whistle, the unmistakable alarm of fading vital signs. He meant to silence the machine somehow, in case they came running for him, in case they tried to save him, but instead slipped in the puddle of his own blood. He pulled down the monitor—dropped the blade, heard it clatter against the floor—and fell hard on his hip.

With a final effort he ripped free the clinging mask, which now flapped loose and rubbery over his mouth. He was free. His vision returned, and with it the light of the room. He saw everything as it truly was, the sunken world beyond the blinding illness. The light was everywhere all at once, and as he pulled away it became smaller, smaller still, until it split into two gleaming glass cubes. He saw them there, as if from above, felt himself drifting away into depthless space, finally and wholly free of the fear of losing himself.

DREAMS FROM THE DARKLANDS

WHEN SHE WAS SLEEPING, I tattooed skulls on the backs of her kneecaps in blue ink, I told her that if she didn't wake soon I'd have to send round a horse for her in the morning.

Wake soon, I said, you'll want to because the horses round here are not afraid of showing you their teeth.

Still she slept soundly and I don't know why this should be a surprise. Our whole time together I've only ever seen the back of her head, the pale skin crawling with blood-bloated fleas in the part of her hair. Her eyes, when she had them, I've always imagined to look milky and endless like galaxies.

* * *

I woke here, in a field covered in blood, naked and with fingernails brittle, yellow, as long and curled as empty spiral shells washed ashore the black-sand beach, scorched.

Plodding through the blood field, veins flooding with each aortal pump of my legs, heavy breath heaving—I first remember feeling fear here on the day of my awakening.

Why I woke and she hasn't I can't say for sure.

* * *

There is a man, a neighbor of ours, whose house is a giant human face. When he comes home at night, the giant human face opens its dark mouth and allows the man inside.

The neck, shoulders, body, legs, and feet of the house are buried beneath the ground. They stay room temperature all year round. At least, this is what our neighbor tells us, leaning his elbow on our fence, smiling, eyes drowned in ink.

Our neighbor spends most of his free time in the house's stomach, picking through the things he finds. When he puts his ear to the wall, he can hear the house sigh.

The giant human face has no expression on its face. Its cheeks hang low, its brow smooth. Its lips are red, cracked, ulcerated. At night, its dormer windows, when lit, are visible from a distance.

Our neighbor stores the things he has accrued throughout life in the house's attic. He does not label the boxes and often worries that he has let things grow too cluttered. Sometimes he comes over to our yard and leans his elbow on our fence and asks if maybe we'd like to come over and take some of what's his.

I've got no need for things anymore, he says. Not so long as the sky stays dark.

* * *

The horses round here run wild at night, their sweat-gleaned muscles rolling

and glistening in the purple moonlight, their brandished teeth gnashing clacks, strings of flesh hanging loose like forgotten floss. Their eye sockets are empty caves of unexplored darkness and decay, white worms lining their walls.

I think there are moles digging tunnels beneath the blood fields. I think that's

how the grass stays so alive, fed by the pumping of the blood.

* * *

When she wakes up I plan on taking her to where the land ends, to the endless maw at the end of my property—the humming maw. There is a blackness there that bleeds into darker shades of black, a blackness that feels alive and crawling. I feel it in my heart—this is the place for her. This is where I'd like to bring her, once she wakes up.

* * *

This place is a familiar place, a place I remember from my dreams.

You can take me there and throw me over the edge, she says, grinding her teeth facedown into her pillow, voice a muffled whimper. Jump in with me and hold my hand, she says.

That way we'll be together forever. And on the way down we'll be able to see the moon, getting smaller and smaller, hanging like a dinner plate in the sky, a giant face, the man in the moon—a home for all the little green moon men crawling on the surface, tunneling below the low lights.

* * *

And so I wait. Some days I can't even see my hand in front of my face.

That's how dark it can get.

STARGAZER

ILYA FOLLOWED HIS FATHER'S hobbled gait into the corpse-strewn battlefield. The trembling sun radiated clean white heat, and his father's shadow was long and slender, grazing the ashen tangles of the dead and dying, the occasional swollen belly of a horse, its legs oddly straightened. They searched for the gleam of silver—the blades of saber swords, the heads of war axes, breast plates, chain mail, and helmets—anything that could be melted down or reused. His father carried their meager findings in a cloth sack slung over his shoulder, its contents clacking with each step, as well as a walking stick, its end whittled to a point, to assist his deformed leg, the result of a terrible fever weathered in childhood.

The stench of death was enough to make Ilya sick, both sweet and rotten, the phlegm lodged thick in his throat. He had done as his father said and covered his nose and mouth with clean linen, cinched it tight behind his neck. Still the smell was overpowering.

Two days and three nights had passed since the tsar's cavalry had charged the Polish army—since the raging fires died down to smoldering heaps, pale ghosts, the fumes of scorched flesh, the greedy caws of peckish birds of prey—and though a great many of the wounded had succumbed to their injuries, still others cried out for help, exhausted voices near and far, raspy with thirst. Whole heaps of bodies were pinned by hundreds of wooden arrows. Others had been badly chewed by musket balls.

One of the men managed to close a meaty hand around Ilya's leg, just above his ankle. The boy cried out, surprised more than anything else, his voice reedy in the wind. He saw that the soldier's legs were crushed, pinned beneath the rent and collapsed bodies of perhaps a dozen others. He wore the red-dyed fabric and chain mail of the tsar's army, caked in mud. Two of his fingers were missing, severed just above the knuckle, clotted with black blood, and one of his eyes was badly damaged, milky with cataract. Half his teeth had been knocked out, his jaw dislodged and hanging slack. Ilya screamed again, struggling to free himself, and the injured man lunged forward with his other arm, grabbing a fistful of the boy's tattered clothing. In that moment, Ilya saw the flash of a small gold chain wrapped round the man's hand—some sort of family heirloom, perhaps. His pulse quickened.

Ilya felt his father's hand on his arm, felt himself yanked free. The injured man was no match for a test of strength. Ilya's father slapped his son across the face, knocking the boy down, then stood over him, leaning on his stick. These men were beyond saving, he said. Lost souls forsaken by their god. His father drew back—Ilya turned away, covered his eyes—and sank the sharpened end of his long walking stick into the man's throat, grimacing as he leaned his weight into it. There was a gurgling sound, like a cold spring pushing up through layers of mud.

When it was done, and his father turned away, Ilya ripped free the gold chain from the soldier's grasp, then secreted it away deep in his loose, blood-sopped clothing, where not even the flies could befoul it. It was his and his alone. His father could not be trusted with a treasure so valuable. His father was weak; he would sell it to the first buyer, no matter who it might be, any common thief on the side of the road, and spend the money on drink, on women, on games of chance. Ilya, on the other hand, would sell the medal to a nobleman in town, someone with taste, with means, and buy a horse with the earnings, which he would then ride into a new life far away from this terrible war, from the fighting, from his father.

* * *

The general's sprawling camp had been hastily staked along the banks of a quiet river, just over a grassy hill at the edge of the battlefield. The air here was still, and the tsar's red banners, raised high on wooden poles, hung slack. A number of carriage wagons listed awkwardly, their large wooden wheels sunken in the soft mud, and the fleshy-toothed mutts cooped up inside their cages scraped and gnashed at the metal bars. A few skinny horses lowered their fly-swarmed heads, drank greedily from the murky river waters, flicking their thinning tails. Restless men both in and out of uniform—marksmen troops, mainly—clustered beneath canvas tents, drinking steins of cider and stout.

Beyond all of this, tucked away within a tent beneath an ancient oak tree, the general himself stood over piles of yellowed maps spread across a table. Behind him two men stood sentry before a covered wagon, its warped and sun-bleached bed piled high with plump sacks of grain.

Ilya's father approached the table, where the general leaned forward on both hands, seemingly deep in thought. He unslung the cloth sack, let it drop to his feet, and then plunged his blood-stained walking stick into the soft ground, where it remained upright. The general looked up warily; he was a formidable man with watery blue eyes, a long and tangled beard that fell over his unbuttoned coat. He sifted through the odd fragments, careful not to cut himself on their jagged edges, each item seemingly more tarnished than the last, moving a few of the larger pieces into a pile on his right—the bits of blade, the head of an axe, fragments of plate—the others into a pile on his left—the buttons, the buckles, the links of chain. "That's all?"

Ilya's father grunted in response, spat.

The general was unfazed. "I suppose I don't have to remind you that any and all items recovered from the field of battle belong to the grand prince of Moscow."

Ilya closed his small hand over the chain hidden in the folds of his clothing. He felt the blood in his neck like a snake slithering in its skin, ready to shed. Surely the tsar had enough treasures of his own. He wouldn't miss this one tiny, insignificant bit of gold.

His father grunted once more. "We're tired and we're hungry."

The general nodded. He spoke in a solemn voice over his shoulder: "Pay the man."

The soldier nearest the covered wagon struggled with one of the sacks of grain, which he callously slung onto the table, as if it were a corpse.

"The Lord thanks you for your service," the general said.

"Praised be," Ilya's father said. He wrapped his arms around the heavy bag of grain, hoisted it over his shoulder with a strained sigh, leaning heavily on his stick with his free arm, and led the way through the camp, one agonizing step at a time.

The sky was turning dark. In the center of the camp, a bonfire raged, its bright yellow flames wild and high. The soldiers formed a ring around the fire, stripped down to their tunics and trousers, their huddled bodies black silhouettes against the light.

As he maneuvered through the dense crowd, Ilya heard the soldiers jeer and whistle. He watched as the crowd parted wide, letting through two uniformed soldiers who dragged along a listless man. The man's head hung slack, the hair covering his face dripping thick globs of blood, and the tops of his bruised and battered feet dragged shallow ruts in the mud. "So they've rounded him up then," someone said. "Stretch him out," said another. "Lowly coward," said a third. Laughter rippled through the crowd, a cruel laughter, bitter and starved for entertainment.

The soldiers marched their prisoner toward the full-summer bloom of the oak tree, its massive foliage swaying in the early-evening shadow. The restless, murmuring crowd closed in on the prisoner, lifted him on outstretched arms, held him aloft on a bed of hands. He seemed to float there for a moment, mercifully unconscious, arms opened wide. And then—with a resounding cheer—a black rope tied into a noose swung up into the air and around one of the mighty oak's low branches.

"Likely a deserter rounded up in the woods," Ilya's father said, "and surely not the only one they'll find, I tell you. I imagine the trees are filled with the cowards, hiding away in every hollow."

Once more, Ilya turned away. He couldn't bear to watch what happened next.

* * *

Into the night they followed the winding, muddy banks of the river, keeping the woods on their left. Few stars shone, and those that did seemed to fade low.

By the time they reached the clearing, the moon shone high. The village huts were shuttered and dark. No smoke rose from their thatched roofs. No one came to greet them upon their return. Even the packs of mangy dogs, usually vigilant during the nighttime hours, had curled themselves away out of sight of their masters, no doubt relieved of duty by their hunger.

Ilya's father shouldered open the door to their hut and ducked through the low threshold. He dropped the heavy sack of grain at the foot of the hearth and fell into his bedroll. Ilya closed the door behind him, quietly as he could.

"Tomorrow, we eat," his father said. "Tonight, we sleep."

When he was sure his father was not looking—was in fact truly sleeping—Ilya hid his treasure deep within his filthy, bug-infested bedroll.

That night, he dreamt of a wild horse in an open field. He saw it there, alone, strong as an army. The sky churned gray, the low rumble of a heartbeat. He approached the horse, moving soundlessly, careful not to frighten it, his arm outstretched before him. Only then, mere inches away from running his fingers over the horse's brilliant coat, the beast turned its head. Its eyes were thick with cataracts, its long skull split open, the quivering, discolored tissue inside exposed. And though the horse still breathed, each time it did so its ribs widened, showing rotting meat clinging to the blue and gray bones, its insides a wild nest of frantic and crawling insects. Recoiling in disgust, Ilya pulled away his hand, only to watch in horror as the horse turned and galloped into the distance, its footfalls entirely silent.

* * *

Ilya woke in the dead of night. Almost without thinking, he rolled over and slid his hand beneath his bedroll, fully expecting the cool touch of the gold chain, his treasure. In its place, however, there was nothing. He looked to his father's bedroll: it was empty.

He quickly found his father's tracks, identifiable by the wide swing of his deformed leg, the pinched hole of his walking stick, and followed them back to the bank of the river, where the trail disappeared into the unruly growth of the forest.

The air was different beneath the forest canopy, as if the woods themselves were alive, hiding away the rustlings and labored breathing of furtive beasts, the haunting laugher of owls. The night was hot and suffocating as a heavy cloak.

Ilya quickly became scared, lost his footing, and slid into a low valley roiling with glowing moon-fog. The terrain behind him was slippery, steep; there was no going back that way. Before him, to his left, his right, he saw only swirling gray mist slatted by the shadowy stretches of tall trees.

He pricked his ears. Far in the distance he heard the unmistakable sound of voices, the voices of men, murmuring low. Perhaps one of them was his father.

He stepped carefully on the soft forest floor, careful not to make too much noise. From deep within the swirls of mist emerged the crooked frame of a decrepit hunting cabin, its windows blacked in shadow, its sagging roof half-collapsed, and its crumbling chimney little more than a sloping pile of stone. The place had a haunted air about it, conjuring images from tales of deep-woods crones, the kind who liked to feast on the flesh of lost children.

He snapped a twig beneath his foot, the sound as loud as musket fire in the still woods. The wooden door of the cabin swung open and clapped against the outside wall, and a hulking form was immediately upon Ilya, grabbing a fistful of the boy's hair and dragging him inside kicking and screaming.

"Speak," said his assailant, "and speak swift or I'll snap your neck. Who are you?"

The boy covered the back of his head with his hands, whimpering, and scrambled up against the wall in the corner of the room. A moment later, someone fixed a candle within a glass lantern that hung from a post in the center of the room. The warm light flooded the darkness. Two men stood before him, both of whom wore the tsar's red uniform.

One man pulled shut the cabin's door, turned, and leaned against it, the features of his face lost in shadow, while the other came close, knelt before the boy. In one swift motion he grabbed a fistful of Ilya's hair and jerked his head back, while simultaneously freeing a dagger from his boot, the edge of which bit into the soft flesh of the boy's throat.

"Speak, I said, or else I'll lash the dirt with your blood."

"The poor boy's terrified," said the other, his voice faint. "Look how he shakes. Let go of him."

The man hesitated a moment, then seemed to heed his compatriot's advice, grunting in frustration before releasing Ilya's hair, removing the blade's edge from his skin. He stood up and turned his back to the boy, facing the other soldier. Ilya pulled air deep into his lungs, his head swimming with relief, fear, and excitement. The room smelled of rotting flesh, rotting wood, blood and soil. The two men kept their voices low, arguing in the shadows.

"He's seen our faces," said the one.

"He's just a boy."

"You underestimate the young. They know more than they let on."

The quiet one stepped closer. Ilya saw that his face was ashen, that he breathed shallowly, and cradled his stomach with one arm, his fingers stained with blood. Even in that moment, in the low light, Ilya knew that this man was not long for this world. Perhaps that was why he found it easy to be merciful.

"Don't worry," the wounded man said. He smiled, showing blood-stained teeth. "My name is Alexei. My friend goes by Leo. What do they call you?" His slow, yellow eyes studied the boy intently.

Ilya said nothing, too scared to move, to speak, to even draw breath.

"We can be friends, can't we?" asked Alexei. "My friend meant no harm. You merely startled us here, alone in these dark woods. You'll forgive him?"

Still Ilya said nothing.

Ilya's mind returned to the horse from his dream, feeling once more the dread of uncovering the animal's decay. And yet, as he turned these sights over in his mind, they began to unravel, any memory of the rotting horse soon evaporating into nothingness, peeling away like layers of onionskin.

A feeling of hopelessness came over him as sudden as fever, eating away at his insides. He was tired and hungry and lost. He'd been abandoned by his father. He'd lost his treasure. Before he could stop it his whole body was wracked by the force of his sobbing.

"Come now," Alexei said. "There is no need for that. You can wait here with us. We'll keep you safe. Tell me, do you like stories? Yes, I see that got your attention. Perhaps you'd like to hear a story to pass the time?" The soldier leaned against the post in the center of the room, coughed once more and slid slowly to the floor, still cradling his wound. His voice had a faraway sound to it, as if he were reciting a dream. "Have you heard the tale of the two angels? It's a tale my mother used to tell me when I was your age. It remains close to my heart."

Leo sighed loudly, turned to face one of the windows.

"These two angels lived together in the sky above the world and had done so for all of time," Alexei said. "One of the angels had white wings and the other black, and though they were brothers, they shared no love. The white-winged angel chose to keep his eyes on the world below, where he could watch over the doings of man. He loved to watch man build his ingenious cities, create new life, and obey the word of God. Because he filled his days with the good in life, he was in turn filled with compassion. The black-winged angel, on the other hand, chose to gaze at the stars above, where he could ponder the great mysteries of all of creation. What thrives out there in the deep dark, he wondered. What is the meaning of existence? He cared not for man or for the sanctity of life because he saw only the chaos of the outer dark. He contemplated only what could never be known."

The solider coughed, spat blood. "So you see the white-winged angel understood that life is precious, that it must be protected, whereas the black-winged angel saw only the slow death of the stars." He coughed again, and when he continued, he could barely be heard. His lower lip quivered. "Now, boy, what if I told you that a man was tasked to fight in a war he believed immoral? What if I told you that he was tasked with fighting alongside Cossacks? Or that he was commanded to kill those born in Poland, when so much of our blood is shared? Would you think him a coward for choosing compassion?"

Alexei's eyelids had grown heavy and his breathing had slowed. Suddenly his head hung low and he slumped forward, slipping from the wooden post, black blood running over his fingers and fanning out across the dusty floor.

It took only a moment of silence for Leo to realize that something was amiss. He stormed across the room, knelt before his compatriot, and as he did so, Ilya summoned all of his courage and darted to the door. Leo roared and lunged for the boy, who narrowly avoided his grasp. Ilya flung wide the wooden door and flew headlong into the dark of the woods.

* * *

Ilya entered the camp and didn't recognize where he was until the star-littered sky opened wide and trembling above him, until he smelled once more the brackish and muddy stink of the river. Acrid waves of smoke from the yellow fires rolled over the clearing, thick enough to choke on, and throngs of men reeking of cider and pork grease stood arm in arm, swaying and bellowing like wild beasts, their flushed faces shining red and demonic in the firelight. No one seemed to notice Ilya as he pushed his way through the crowds, drawn to the mighty oak tree and its magnificent blue foliage.

There, among the others who had been judged guilty, Ilya saw his father hanging from the tree's lowest branch, rope cinched round his broken neck, his face fat and purple, arms bound behind his back. The wind turned his father's body slightly and Ilya saw that its hands had been severed, wrists stumped by gaping black wounds—punishment for a thief, or perhaps for a man unwise enough to get caught with something so valuable as gold.

He did not see it right away, floating high above the ground and looking like so much shadow, the play of light against the swaying leaves. No, he did not notice the angel until it wrapped its leathery black wing around his father's corpse, claiming him as one of its own. And then it was gone, just as quickly as it had shown itself, it joined once more with the malicious black night that had birthed it.

Ilya looked up into the stars and saw only an emptiness that threatened to swallow whole the mundane doings of man. How could it be any other way?

He entered the general's tent and stood there sullen and ashamed, unable to lend voice to his demons, as the soldiers who faced him demanded answers to their questions. It wasn't until the general himself stood before the boy, recognizing him as the son of that traitorous and crippled thief, saying just as much, that Ilya looked up, tears in his red-rimmed eyes.

"There is one more who must be killed," Ilya said. "A deserter hiding in a hunting cabin. I'll lead you to him."

In those final still moments of twilight before the blood-red sun rose above the tree line, Ilya made his way once more toward the forest, appearing only as a silhouette to the soldiers who followed him, so many drunk and lumbering fools, his form warped by the light of those madly dancing flames. And then he was gone, welcomed by the dark.

THE SCHOOLMASTER

OUTSIDE THE WINDOW OF my apartment above the apothecary's shop, I overheard a killing in the street below. A seventeen-year-old boy—I later learned he was one of my students, Thomas—was torn apart, by what, we do not know. It was just after midnight.

The local enforcers arrived within minutes, sweeping the street with their torches. I darkened the gas lamps of my room so I could better see through my window. Voices—men and women, children and adults—filled the dust-choked streets, coming from everywhere all at once, threatening retaliation, crying out in despair, confusion, hopelessness. It went on that way for nearly an hour—that insufferable noise—and then went suddenly quiet, replaced by so much daylight, everywhere, as always.

Later that afternoon, the captain of the enforcers announced that the attack on poor Thomas must have been carried out by a pack of wild dogs. There are no other reasonable explanations, he said.

Days have passed. Many strays have been shot on sight, their young bludgeoned. A pile of their charred corpses smolders in the square, unceasing. The howls of their brethren can be heard at all hours, echoing from the black hills surrounding our town. Those who knew and loved Thomas have assembled a small, wood-plank shrine on the walkway where he fell. Hundreds of glass prayer candles glow orange throughout the night. His name is crudely painted on a small plank nailed to a nearby tree.

* * *

Once each year I teach the school children the legend of ancient people who lived in the world of dark. The books I recite my lessons from—bindings broken, leather covers stretched and smooth as river stones—state that the ancients had evolved from a race of cave-dwelling primitives, awful creatures who wore animal skins on their backs and ate their dead to survive the harsh realities of never-ending winter.

Then came the era of light, in which the eaters of the dead mastered fire. They used these flames to light their caves and cook the animals they slayed. At night, fearful of the forest's whispers, the ancients huddled among themselves in their caves, watching the shadows cast from the fire dance across their walls. This play of shadows was mesmerizing—and certain members of their tribes began to stand before the others, translating the shadows, describing what the flames had given them—blessed them—to see, such visions from the beyond.

This birthed the era of knowledge. As generations passed, the ancients handed down memorized stories to their young, much in the same manner I go about my duties with the school children. The flames, they said, were gifted from an all-knowing god who lived in the center of the Earth. The flames were the father of all creation. The world as they understood it blossomed: they soon lit torches to tread through the woods without fear; guided mechanical ships over pools of placid water and through chasms of fog, their voyages intricately logged and uninterrupted; and invented new words to describe and discuss advancements made to their society.

The next step was to write all of this down and bind it in leather. So the knowledge was written. It is here where the horror began.

* * *

Earlier this evening, a meeting was held at our town hall, called for and mediated by the captain of the enforcers. I arrived late and made my way to the front of the room where an empty seat was waiting for me. As I passed, the men bowed their heads and removed their hats. After weeks of careful hunting, the captain said, the packs of wild dogs had at last been exterminated. The citizens of our fair town should no longer fear leaving our homes during the nighttime hours. Never again, he said, will we lose another innocent child to the bloodlust of beasts.

And yet, later that very night, I was roused from my slumber once more—the orange light of the harvest moon filling my room—to the sound of a woman pleading for help. Her son, she screamed, her son had been murdered, torn apart by the dogs.

The men of our town, aided by their firstborn sons, stormed the hills, armed with whatever they could find: scythes, pitchforks, axes. Whole patches of forest were razed. By the time the morning sun slugged into the pale sky, the streets of our town were fogged with the stench of smoke.

Even though no more dogs had been found, the naked and whipped body of the captain swung from a rope in the town's square, hanged high for all to see. Somebody, the townsfolk said, perhaps only repeating what they had heard, somebody had to be held accountable for the most recent killing. Who better than the man who had stood before us and promised it would never happen again?

* * *

If you listen closely to the sounds of the night, you will hear the soft treading of ghosts—the children say this with firm voices. They say this to spook one another, even though my school has firm rules in place against the telling of such tall tales. Where it comes from, I'll never know. It certainly does not come from me. And so it is my job to shush them, to administer punishment—twenty lashes of the stick for each untruth told—and make examples of the worst of them. What else can be done?

Each morning they move past me in a silent line, heads down, filing into the schoolhouse, empty vessels ready to be filled with knowledge. When the youngest of them is safely inside and has taken his seat, I close the heavy double doors. There, in that austere and mannered silence, we begin our lessons.

THE GUTTER AT THE BOTTOM OF THE WORLD

IT WASN'T UNTIL THE skinny tires of Kate's Honda scraped against the curb, after she hit the flashers and slammed the door behind her, only then, in the smog-warm night, with the phased sounds of sirens rising and falling, did she think, please, not another lost and lonely girl. Deep down, though, she knew that this was the real world, and in the real world things were almost always as bad as she feared.

They fell into place that night the way they often did, those bad things, the crime scene—the colors, the noise—the carnival-like chaos of it all. The blue and red police lights spun against the drab North Hollywood street, a corridor of crowded apartment complexes, barred windows and sickly palms. Taut strands of yellow caution tape boxed out the throng of onlookers, a few old ladies smoking cigarettes, a horde of filthy skater trash, a yuppie couple in matching khaki shorts walking a yipping Yorkie. And on the other side of the tape, two uniformed cops standing shoulder to shoulder—both holding the collars of their thick vests, as cops often seemed inclined to do—barking at people to stay back, to put away their cellphones, move along, disperse.

Kate threaded her way through the crowd until the scene was only a few feet away. There, on the pavement between two parked cars, she saw a thin, pale arm sticking out from beneath a blood-soaked sheet. She snapped a quick photo with the camera on her phone, using her thumb and forefinger to zoom in, frame the shot. Then she pressed the thumbnail to enlarge the image. It filled the screen, a smear of nebulous red light, the arm limp and lifeless yet not devoid of a discomfiting beauty—the neck of a strangled swan.

She looked up from the screen and saw one of the cops take a few assertive strides her way, looking pissed off, boots chunking against the pavement—the camera flash must have caught his attention. Kate tapped the home button, then the record button on her phone's voice recorder, opened the notepad app. Her movements were made without thought, pure muscle memory.

"No photos," the cop said, close now and pointing a gloved finger. "I won't tell you again."

Kate pretended like she hadn't heard. She extended her arm toward the cop, held out her phone like it was a mic, her voice in competition with the noise of the crowd, the sirens. "What happened here?"

The cop's eyes narrowed. A thin white scar pinched the skin over one of his eyebrows and ran straight back over the curve of his shaved head, pitted skin gleaming in the streetlight glow. His earlobe on that side was missing a chunk of flesh. And his cruel smile showed small and sharp teeth like a piranha—similarly cold, unfeeling eyes. All of these things—these details she'd been trained to pick out, make note of—made Kate's skin crawl. Without missing a beat, the cop snatched the phone out of Kate's hand, dropped it to the ground, and sent it skidding across the pavement with a swing of his boot.

Now it was her turn to be pissed off. "I'm a reporter with Clued-In-LA," she said, her voice a bit more shrill than she would have liked. She looked to her left, her right, hoping someone was recording this, getting it on the record, but no one seemed to have noticed. No one seemed to care. "You can't do that."

"Do what?" the cop said, turning away. A moment later, two more cars rolled onto the scene, a cruiser calling its siren and an unmarked black sedan spinning silent dash-lights. An ambulance followed, and then a fire truck, God knew why. The cops fanned out into the crowd, throwing their weight around. One of them barked into a megaphone. Next thing she knew Kate was back in her Honda, windows down, cutting the muggy night air along a dry stretch of highway, tears of frustration blurring the sea of shifting taillights. She headed home because there was nowhere else to go, no one to go home to. Not tonight, at least. She'd have to come crawling back to North Hollywood in the morning and look for her phone, knowing all along it would be a waste of what little time she had. Fuck it. Her phone was gone. Just another object swallowed up by the cracks that lurked between things, always lying in wait, ready to swallow up some poor, misfortunate soul, so many of the young women in this city, lost and lonely, fresh off the buses from God knew where—grim cornfields and trailer parks, oil-pump desert towns and festering swamps—dreams of stardom blinding them to the dangers grinning their veneers in plain sight.

Kate had a hunch that whatever had happened in North Hollywood that night, there was a story that needed to be told, there almost always was. Maybe this would be like one of those old and sordid Hollywood murders: Black Dahlia, Ronni Chasen, or Christa Helm. That's what her instincts told her, and Kate had long ago learned to trust her instincts.

That's how she'd kept her job at the daily in New York all those years, each more cutthroat than the last, surviving round after round of layoffs. Back then, she was fresh out of Columbia's J-school and looking to make a name for herself. And that was exactly what she had done, racking up bylines, breaking stories about unscrupulous media execs, accusations of sexual harassment—that kind of thing. It was her area of expertise: scumbag men who abused their power. One day, she pissed off the wrong person—she never did find out who it was—and the daily's managing editor sent her packing. Too much of a liability, he'd said, wringing his hands, the gutless piece of shit. She splashed her iced coffee in his face and never looked back.

Now, here she was, on the other side of the country, exiled to a depressing little bungalow in porn-soaked Van Nuys, covering the crime beat for a trashy website that no one even read, churning out content to sell algorithm-determined ad space. It was impossibly meaningless.

Kate cracked open a bottle of cheap chardonnay, plopped down on her couch, and opened her laptop. The first thing she did was check her bank account. She'd have to put the new phone on her credit card, the one that wasn't already maxed out. An unplanned expense was the last thing she needed. There was still so much to take care of around the house. She hadn't even finished unpacking yet. Stacks of boxes lined the walls of every room, labeled in Sharpie: Kitchen, Living Room, Bedroom, Books. It seemed like there was never enough time in the day to get her shit together. Not when there was so much work to be done, so many bills to be paid. It seemed like there was never enough wine left in the bottle. She refilled her glass, took another sip—a longer one this time—and closed her eyes.

The image of the crime scene came back to her, the photo she'd snapped on her phone, an impression that haunted her like the lingering traces of a bad dream. She recalled details—a beaded gold band on one finger, a strange tattoo on another, fingernails painted dark—but it was as if her mind wouldn't let her see what she'd seen. Each time she tried to recall the image it was less detailed somehow, until eventually she couldn't really remember it at all. God, what the fuck was wrong with her?

Maybe it was the temperature. She still wasn't used to the bone-bleaching heat of southern California. With the ceiling fan cranked on high and the overtaxed window unit blaring, the heat in her bungalow was maddening. Ten minutes on the couch and she was sweating through her T-shirt. On the radio they'd said this was the hottest summer in years, and it was supposed to get even hotter. That reminded her: she needed to get the *check engine* light on her car looked at. It had first popped on during the drive from New York, and ever since she'd crossed the desert it was periodically joined by the even more ominous *engine hot* light. It might be a radiator problem—no guessing how much that would cost. She'd just have to add it to the list of unplanned expenses.

She finished her glass of wine and opened a second bottle. It was all so overwhelming sometimes. And there was nothing she could do about it besides click on the same sites again and again, refresh the same pages over and over, looking for breaking news, anything about the murder in North Hollywood. In a separate private-browsing tab she went to Pornhub and scrolled through the BDSM category, not interested in anything too extreme. She mostly liked videos of women humiliating men, using words to inflict pain. Videos like those made her feel like she was in control. Tonight she wanted the opposite. She pressed play, hid the browser window behind the other windows, and listened to the sounds: skin on skin, crying out—that intoxicating mix of pleasure and pain. She wondered how many of the girls in these videos lived in Van Nuys, how many she'd passed on the street, never recognizing them for who they were or what they did to make ends meet.

Kate killed the second bottle of wine. Not long after that, she slipped into a fitful sleep.

* * *

She slept in late the next day, and when she woke she felt energized. No more of this helpless victim bullshit. Today, she was going to take control of her life. She was going to do what she did best: follow her instincts and find the story. Kate made a pitcher of cold-brew coffee, sat at the small table in her tiny, sunbaked kitchen, and got to work.

First she called in a favor from a friend of a friend, someone who worked in records for the LAPD, told him she was looking for anything on female DOAs brought in from North Hollywood the night before. She was in luck. It just so happened that the body of a young woman was photo ID'd that morning by her distraught boyfriend, same poor fucker who had reported her missing a week ago.

The victim's birth name was Anastazie Lhotsky—unique enough to get good search results. Kate plugged it into Google. Anastazie was from a small town in Minnesota, some place Kate had never heard of before. She was young, 20 or 21, and beautiful, big green eyes, perfect skin, walnut brown hair. It took a while but Kate confirmed that Anastazie was an actress and model who went by the name Melody Carmichael. From there Kate learned that outside of some photoshoots, mostly tasteful semi-nudes—under yet another name—Carmichael had only a single acting credit, a project titled *The Angel of Death*, which was in postproduction. That information led Kate to an article published in *Variety*, of all places, couldn't get more mainstream than that. Apparently *The Angel of Death* was the long-awaited comeback feature film from reclusive arthouse director Leonard Shea.

This was surprising, to say the least. Shea was a legend. In the late '70s he'd written and directed a deeply unpleasant avant-garde horror flick called *Wormlust* that was now considered a cult classic, still screening in the midnight slot at achingly hip theaters. The film was nearly impossible to describe, pure sensory overload, composed of rhythmic montages that stitched together highly sexualized, surrealistic imagery, writhing piles of bodies slicked in scorched oil, black-hooded ritualized murders, plagues of locusts, surgical footage—all set to a pummeling protoindustrial score. Kate had watched it twice, both times while an undergrad, both times at the whiny urgings of the moody, unwashed men she'd been seeing. She associated the film with the smell of clove cigarettes, the ashen mouthfeel of cheap red wine, and bad memories of fumbling, unfulfilling sex.

Wormlust wasn't Shea's only claim to fame, of course. Years later, he inexplicably advanced to the studio system, where he released exactly one big-budget flop, a bloated, rape-obsessed interpretation of the Bluebeard folktale titled *His Many Wives*. Slapped with an X rating and dropped by its distributor, it was widely considered one of the most misguided films ever made. Shea's investors each lost a small fortune, and he was subsequently banished from Hollywood.

There was no telling where he'd gone after that. Kate searched Google images but couldn't find any photos that were even close to current. The ones that did exist were old, black and white. She studied

Shea's long face. He had rock-star good looks: a wide jaw, razor-sharp cheekbones. In every photo he wore a cowboy hat and mirror shades, a hand-rolled cigarette dangling from his lower lip.

The fact that Carmichael had been cast in one of Shea's films was especially significant. Kate recalled something one of those unwashed young men had told her while screening *Wormlust*, something she'd written off as yet another urban legend. One of the actresses cast in *His Many Wives*—some young woman whose name no one could remember—had been murdered shortly after shooting her scenes. None of her footage was used in the final cut, so the rumor went, but apparently she had played one of Bluebeard's wives, and in the single scene she shot, she was beaten, raped, strangled to death, and hanged on a meat hook. Shea did something like 80 or 100 takes, spent days on this one scene, Bluebeard killing his wife again and again, until this poor actress was decimated physically and mentally, until Shea had what he wanted—a performance of a woman being broken by a man that was totally believable because it was very nearly real, a woman who was so exhausted, so utterly destroyed by her husband's abuses, by the sacrifices required of her, that she was grateful to be killed.

And that wasn't even the worst part. This was the real world, after all—things always got worse. Weeks after this nameless actress's scenes were wrapped her body was supposedly found hanging from a meat hook in an industrial freezer in the Valley. She'd been beaten, raped, and strangled. Who knows, maybe the whole thing was staged for publicity, a fucked-up marketing tactic designed to drum up controversy. Shea certainly enjoyed a dark reputation—then and now. In fact, some of his nuttier fans even went so far as to claim that *Wormlust* contained genuine footage of the netherworld.

Kate typed a couple different phrases into Google but nothing came up. She scoured some message boards, scrolled through a couple of poorly written blogs and Letterboxd reviews, read dozens of archived newspaper articles, but there was nothing to be found about an actress in *His Many Wives* turning up dead. Rumor or not, once was a tragedy, twice was a pattern. Two women cast in Shea's films, both young and inexperienced, both found dead. The coincidence was enough for Kate to go on. She typed up a pitch letter—explaining in careful detail how a recent murder in North Hollywood might be connected to a legendary cult filmmaker—and sent it to Suki, an old friend from J-school, now a senior editor at one of the mass media glossies in New York. Total Hail Mary, but she might as well start at the top.

She looked at the clock on the wall in her kitchen—it was just after two in the afternoon. Her pitcher of cold brew was empty. Feeling good about herself, excited by everything she'd uncovered, Kate threw on some clean clothes and drove over to the T-Mobile shop on Victory Boulevard to pick out a new cellphone. Hell, she deserved it.

After the sales associate booted up the new phone and slid it across the counter, the first thing Kate did was check to see if anything from the previous night had saved to the cloud—the photo of the arm, the voice recording of her interaction with the cop—but she was out of luck on both counts.

Her credit card was still processing when her email account chimed a dozen times over. Among the deluge from her editor at Clued-In-LA, Kate's heart leapt when she saw a response from Suki. She opened the email, could hardly believe what she read. The glossy wanted 3,000 words and, amazingly enough, offered half pay upfront—enough to cover Kate's rent for a month. She'd get the rest when the piece was published. Word on the street was Shea's new film was being screened for private audiences. They might even be able to arrange for Kate to see it. Either way, there would be renewed interest in his work, whatever he'd been up to in the past forty years, and they wanted the piece ready to run by the time the new film came out. Kate fired back an email accepting the job. Suki's next email had the contract attached.

Half an hour later, stuck in traffic on her way home, air-conditioner blaring, Kate got a call. The area code was 442—somewhere out in the desert. She put the call on speakerphone.

"I am glad to have reached you, Miss Murphy," said the woman on the line, her voice velvety, etched with age, the barely noticeable trace of an Eastern European accent.

"Please, call me Kate. How can I help you?"

"Kate, of course. My name is Carol Reid. I am the agent of Leonard Shea. It has been brought to my attention that you are writing a story about my client. This is correct? I do make it a point to know these things. Please, you must accept my apologies for contacting you so urgently. Mr. Shea is—how do I say this?—quite protective of his reputation. He is a particular man. Very particular. As such, he would like very much to meet you—to give you an exclusive interview, of course. That's right. Mr. Shea will tell you everything you desire to know. I'm sure you have many questions. Today, if possible. You are in Los Angeles, yes? Splendid. I will text you the address. You do not mind driving a ways, I hope? We are in Barstow. Yes, we look forward to meeting with you too."

This was certainly unexpected, but Kate didn't question it—she couldn't afford to. There was no hesitating in moments like this. She would do anything for a story, or so she told herself, as she plugged Shea's address into her GPS, pulled off at the nearest exit, and changed course.

* * *

The drive to Barstow took just under three hours. Kate's Honda hummed through the oppressive, concrete sprawl of the city, emerging as the road straightened into a limitless stretch of highway, waves of oily heat rippling the dust-choked horizon. As she drove, she listened carefully to the sound of the car's engine, eager to avoid breaking down out in the wastelands. Whenever the *engine hot* light blinked on, Kate pulled off into the nearest gas station, bought some water, and collected her thoughts. She watched the turkey vultures circle some unknown meal in the distance.

There were so many things she wanted to ask Shea. Of course, she'd have to wait for just the right moment to bring up Carmichael. The trick was getting him to where she needed him. She spoke into the voice recorder on her phone, rehearsing and refining the questions she planned on asking, interrupted intermittently by the GPS telling her when to turn.

Eventually she reached an intricately designed driveway gate, something Shea apparently felt was necessary way out here in the middle of nowhere, no name even on the map. A sleek black camera mounted on one of the gate pillars zeroed in on Kate's window. The gate buzzed, opened. She followed the winding gravel driveway up to a large ranch house.

The place was gorgeous, fit for the cover of *Dwell.* The landscaping was immaculate, scattered with small stones and picturesque cacti. The driveway was hand-laid slabs of gray stone. And the house itself was an elegant mix of stacked stonework and adobe, all long lines and large windows. Gaslight lamps mounted over the wide front door glowed pleasantly orange, exuding warmth, especially inviting in the cool, early evening air.

Kate knocked softly and the door opened, revealing a young woman in expensive athleisure, her flaxen hair pulled into a high ponytail. She couldn't have been a day older than eighteen, with model-thin arms, delicate features. She let Kate inside, snapping her gum, and promptly slipped away.

"Hello?" Kate said, her voice echoing in the foyer. The house was immense, a symmetrical progression of rooms, frames within frames, low lamplight, dark wood, glass, and stone. The air smelled sweetly of incense. She heard the distant sound of running water.

A handsome older woman wearing a tailored dress suit stepped out of the shadows, extending her hand. Silver bracelets clattered on her wrist. Her stylish hair was cut short. The woman introduced herself as Carol Reid. Kate returned her smile, took Carol's hand in hers, shocked by its roughness, the sturdiness of leather and bone.

Carol's heels clicked against the polished floors as she led Kate deeper into the house. They descended some short staircases, turned a few corners, passing overflowing bookshelves and a gurgling fountain, went down a long hall, and entered an impressive great room, its raftered ceiling maybe twenty feet high, shrouded in shadow. The lights were dimmed. A series of full-length windows overlooked a large patio and swimming pool—its waters a pristine, sapphire blue—beyond which stretched the limitless desert. In the pool, a woman in a one-piece bathing suit was swimming laps, her stroke measured and strong. Kate wondered idly if it was the same girl who had opened the front door, but didn't think so.

Leonard Shea sat in the center of a huge leather wraparound couch. He slung one long leg over the other, arms out at his sides, resting atop the cushions. He wore gray Levis, a white V-neck T-shirt, and a canvas cowboy hat, the brim pulled low over his eyes. He was barefoot.

Carol took a seat near Shea. She sat up perfectly straight, impeccable posture, and smoothed her skirt over her thighs. She gestured to the opposite side of the couch, instructed Kate to make herself at home. And when she did, as soon as Kate sat down, a young woman in a black dress swooped in out of nowhere—another pretty little thing, this one raven-haired, stick thin—and placed a sweating bottle of Pellegrino on a coaster. How many of these girls were there? Before Kate could even say thank you, the raven-haired beauty was gone, disappearing around some dark corner.

"Again, thank you so much for driving all this way," Carol said. "Mr. Shea certainly appreciates being given the opportunity to speak to you directly—and on such short notice." She turned to Shea, who tipped the brim of his hat with two fingers.

"Howdy," he said, voice shockingly deep.

"It's an honor," Kate said, studying Shea closely. His forearms were toned, fingers slender. She recognized that long face. He looked as if he hadn't aged a day since those old black-and-white photos. Though it was difficult to make out his eyes beneath the cowboy hat, he was still handsome.

Then Kate saw something that took her breath away. Hanging low on a leather-cord necklace Shea wore a silver pendant bearing a strange symbol—a ring with a cross at its apex. She couldn't believe it. That was it—the thing she couldn't remember—the thing she'd seen at the crime scene in North Hollywood. Suddenly it clicked: it was the same symbol that was tattooed on Melody Carmichael's finger.

All the questions Kate had so carefully rehearsed during the drive went up in smoke. Still, she opened the voice recorder app and placed her phone on the glass coffee table. "Do you mind if I record our conversation? I thought maybe we'd start with some casual stuff before we get to your new film." She pointed at Shea's necklace. "That's an interesting design. Can you tell me a bit about that?"

Shea looked down at the pendant, as if he was surprised to see it there, eyes hidden beneath the brim of his hat. "It's the sigil of the abyss," he said, looking up slowly, speaking calmly. "I like it out here in the desert because the climate is unforgiving. It's boiling hot during the day, freezing cold at night. The kinds of things that grow out here cover themselves in spikes. Little things get eaten by big things. That's what this symbolizes—this necklace. They say the abyss is a place of extremes. Sandstorms, lava, mountains of flesh." He paused. "There's life everywhere, you know, so long as you know how to find it. In the desert, it's hidden away. It's adapted."

Something about the way he spoke, the words he chose, scraped at Kate's nerves. He was so serious. There was no detectable irony in his voice, no sarcasm, no recognizable emotion. He spoke with the fanatical conviction of a true believer. She looked around the room. It was dark, but she was still able to make out a series of large, oil-based paintings on the wall behind Shea. The paintings seemed to portray elaborate scenes of the apocalypse, orgies of full-bodied female nudes and black-winged demons, hardened phalluses, rivers of gore. The images in these paintings brought to mind what little she remembered of *Wormlust.*

"What can you tell me about those?" Kate said, motioning to the wall.

Shea didn't react. Carol, however, looked over her shoulder before turning back to Kate. "The paintings? They are beautiful, are they not? That's how Mr. Shea supports himself when he is not making his films. Many do not know this. You should put it in your article. Mr. Shea is a great maker of art. Fine art. He is very accomplished. Those are his most recent pieces. They go for a high price. In fact, we are currently finalizing their sale to a well-known collector, the owner of the studio financing Mr. Shea's latest film, nonetheless. A powerful man. He is a great fan."

Shea cut in. "Those paintings are special. They show the demon Abaddon as he presides over the realm of the dead. The black-winged angel. King of the locusts."

Kate steered the conversation away from this talk of demons and apocalypse. She told herself it was because she didn't know how much time she had, but really it was because she was uncomfortable, thrown off her game. They spent the next few minutes talking about Shea's frustrations with the formalities of the art world, how he passed his days out here in the desert, waking up late, only eating a single meal each day, exploring the land. He talked about the energy vortices he had discovered, his experiments with dark crystals and peyote, and why he refused to read any books. Kate was relieved to find that, after its menacing start, the interview evolved into something more comfortable, conventional even. She began to find Shea strangely alluring, laughing at his cryptic comments. All the while, Carol kept smiling, broadcasting her approval.

Outside, it was quite dark. The sky had turned a beautiful, deep shade of desert-rose purple. The patio lights kicked on and the pool gleamed bright as a polished gem. As Shea spoke about his admiration for lizards, Kate watched as the woman swimming laps emerged from the water—a silhouette against the blinding lights—ascending the steps in the pool's shallow end. She bent over, shook out her hair, and wrapped her willowy legs in a towel. Then she opened the sliding glass door and entered the room.

At first, Kate thought she must be mistaken, that what she saw was impossible. It had to be impossible. The girl who had just entered the room was identical to Melody Carmichael—same green eyes, flawless skin, and walnut brown hair. But it couldn't be Melody Carmichael. Melody Carmichael was dead.

Shea stopped talking, perhaps sensing that Kate was no longer listening.

"I see you are struck by the beauty of my newest client," Carol said to Kate. "This is Bianca Rhoads. Soon she will be a big star." She turned to the girl. "Don't be shy, dear. Miss Murphy is a writer. She's here to write an article about Mr. Shea."

"How do you do?" Bianca said, blushing. Her voice was youthful and pure. She kept her eyes trained on the floor.

Kate couldn't imagine how to answer. The question was phrased so formally. She was vaguely aware of the fact that her mouth hung open. She closed it, tried to pull herself together. She was just about to respond when Shea cut in.

"This girl is the bravest actress I have ever worked with. Not like the others. Most actors, most actresses, they never really learn how much bravery it takes to truly let go. To experience one's own death over and over again—that is the ultimate artistic expression. It's the ultimate expression of life itself, all of our experiences in this life. It's a kind of bravery that most people will never be able to imagine. They'll never know what it means to live in that moment, as terrifying as it might be, captured on film, the moment that lasts forever—even if it means embodying your worst fears." As he spoke, his voice grew louder, swelling with something like pride. "Bianca Rhoads will live forever on the screen as somebody else. To really make it as an actress requires..." He searched for the right word. "It requires sacrifice."

Shea stood up, shockingly thin, skeletal, and crept toward Bianca, moving like a cartoon villain, raising his knees high with each step—towering over her. He lightly touched her under her chin, tilting her head back, directing her to gaze into his eyes. Then he craned his neck, leaned forward, and whispered something in her ear, the brim of his cowboy hat brushing aside her damp hair. Then she was gone, skipping happily down the hall at the end of the room, one of its many doors clicking shut behind her.

Kate couldn't help herself. It was too much to hold in any longer. She just blurted it out. "Does the name Melody Carmichael mean anything to you?" It was like all of the air was sucked out of the room. "She was murdered a few days ago. That symbol you wear around your neck, I saw it tattooed on one of her fingers."

Once again, Shea did not seem to react to her question. Carol's smile had disappeared.

Kate couldn't stop now. She couldn't help herself. "That girl," she said, "the one you just introduced to me as Bianca Rhoads? She looks exactly like Melody Carmichael."

Shea was suddenly ferocious. "Tell me, Miss Murphy," he said, growling the words, "where do you think your soul goes once you die? You don't deign to know, do you? Well, let me tell you this, those who are forgotten are banished to unnamed layers of existence—the gutter at the bottom of the world. How does that sound to you?"

Carol nearly leapt to her feet, playing interference, positioning herself between Shea and Kate. "I'm afraid that's all the time we have for today," she said, putting a hand on Shea's shoulder. He shook free of her, ignoring her, crossed the room and stood over Kate. She tried to sink deeper into the couch, staring up at him. No matter what, she couldn't let him know that she was scared. She would not give him the satisfaction of allowing herself to be intimidated.

"Here is what you should put in your fucking article," Shea said. "Here's your fucking lede. This is what you came out here for, right? People like you, you think making films is about creating art, or you think it's about making money. You're fucking clueless. Nothing more than worms—all of you. I've been trying to show you the truth. But you're all too fucking stupid to see it for what it is. When you watch my films, what you see up on that screen, it's more real than you'll ever realize." He raised his arms out to his sides. "I set people free with my camera. The people in my movies, the person who plays the character, they cease to exist. Once you train the lens on a person, they disappear. But the worms lust after violence. They demand it. So I show them what they want to see. I show them other people—people just like them, normal people, like you—getting torn to shreds by monsters. I show them a vision of what it's like to die a painful death, to be cast away and forgotten, and they worship me for it. They elevate me above others. But murder? No, not as you understand it."

Carol wrapped an arm around Shea's thin waist. "I'm afraid you're going to have to see yourself out, Miss Murphy," she said, pulling the famous director away. She guided Shea toward the hall at the far end of the room. His whole body began to shake, as if he were having a seizure.

Kate immediately got up and followed. "Wait," she said, "we're not through here. You can't just yell at me like that and walk away. Where are you going?"

Shea and his agent rushed through the doorway just as Kate caught up with them. And in that moment, she got just a glimpse of the room beyond, its various couches and chairs filled with dozens of women, all in various forms of repose—some wearing robes, others in lingerie, still others wearing nothing at all—their big eyes on Shea, utterly adoring. And then the door slammed shut. Kate instinctively grabbed the handle. It was locked. She banged on the door, but no one answered. She was so mad, so utterly bewildered by what had just happened, she stormed back into the great room, and, not knowing what else to do with her anger, her confusion, picking up the still-full bottle of Pellegrino, cried out, and shattered it against the wall.

* * *

She didn't get home until midnight. The whole drive back, all she could think about was that room full of women, looking like hungry cats pleading to be fed. Was she supposed to see that? Was it just a wild publicity scheme?

Back in her bungalow, Kate turned on all the lights, cranked the ceiling fan, and opened a bottle of wine. Whatever it was Shea was raving about—setting people free, giving the worms what they wanted to see, being worshipped—she couldn't make any sense of it.

There was no way that had been Melody Carmichael, either. It couldn't have been. Kate opened her laptop, took down half her glass of wine in two mouthfuls, and typed Carmichael's name into Google. There it was—an article in the *Times* reporting her death. Kate studied the photo of Carmichael at the top of the page. She really did look exactly like the girl who had been doing laps in the pool at Shea's house. And yet, the more she stared at the photo, the less she was able to see her. It was as if Carmichael's face was erasing itself from Kate's perception, one detail at a time. This sense of erasure was the same feeling she'd had when she took the photo of the arm in North Hollywood, when she tried to recall its details later that same night. Something was missing from what she remembered, like there were holes in her memories, draining details.

Kate closed her eyes, listened to the blades of the ceiling fan as they sliced the humid air. She was hotter than ever, stripped off all her clothes. She spent the next few hours drinking glass after glass of wine, letting it dribble down her chin. When she got tired, she locked herself in her bedroom with her laptop.

She went back to Pornhub, scrolled through the videos, and found something rougher than last time, something that looked like it was filmed in an empty warehouse. The girl in the video had a ball gag in her mouth, her arms tied behind her back, ropes crisscrossing her chest. Mascara ran down her face; her eyes looking up at something beyond the frame. She looked just like Carmichael. A man wearing a black hood over his face approached her. Kate didn't want to see this. She went to the next video. This one showed a girl tied to a table getting fucked by a machine. She looked just like Bianca Rhoads. Kate clicked on video after video. All the performers looked scared. They looked like all the girls she passed by on the street. They were girls whose names no one knew—forgotten, overlooked. The videos got weirder. Everyone was slicked in scorched oil, plagues of locusts descending from the sky. Men in black cloaks held one of the girls down and cut open her belly, chanting, carving symbols into her thighs, firelight flickering against the walls. It looked so real. There was so much blood. It didn't look like a performance, the way the girl's skin puckered, the way she recoiled from the bite of the blade, the sounds she made, involuntary and guttural. The men pulled out her organs by the fistful while she screamed. Her eyes remained open wide with fear, disbelief. Her chest heaved with each desperate breath. Kate couldn't help but watch, fascinated, repulsed. Was this for real? She clapped shut her computer, plunging the room into darkness, and wept herself to sleep.

In the morning, she lay in bed and stared at the ceiling. Her head was killing her. Her eyes ached, a dull, pulsing pain. When her phone vibrated, it was as loud as a buzzsaw, ripping maliciously through soft tissue, skull splitting, adrift somewhere in her tangled bedsheets. She dug it out—Barstow area code.

It was Carol. Of course it was Carol. She heard the agent's voice, as genial as ever, apologizing for Shea's outburst, saying something about his medication levels being off. "He's an old man," she said. "He's on pills for the pain. Everyone in Hollywood is on pills. Surely you must know that."

Kate listened quietly, waiting until Carol was finished, and when it was her turn to speak, she said, "Nothing was off the record, you know. I'm going to use his words. Everything he said, whatever it meant. Everything I saw in that house…" She paused. "Whatever it was. I'm going to use it all. I'm going to write about all of it. And if you think it would be helpful for readers to know that Leonard Shea was under the influence of prescription medication during our interview, I'd be happy to include that information as well."

The line was quiet for a few moments. Carol cleared her throat. "Naturally," she said, "you are the professional. You should write the article as you see fit."

"Okay then," Kate said, angling to end the call. She felt like she might throw up, a mixture of nerves and nausea. Her mouth flooded with saliva.

"Just one moment, Miss Murphy. Before you go. There is one last bit of unfinished business. Mr. Shea and I think it is only fair that you attend a private screening of his new film, *The Angel of Death.* Whenever suits you. Mr. Shea will not be there, of course. You will have your privacy. You will watch the film and then decide how you wish to write the article, yes?"

Kate agreed and was more than a little relieved to end the call. Carol was right. As much as she might loathe the idea, Kate had to watch the film. She couldn't finish the article without seeing it. A few minutes later she received a text with the address. She looked it up, some faceless building in an office park in Studio City, a postproduction facility. A second text came in with the number of the viewing room. Kate got out of bed, took a pull from the bottle of vodka she kept in her freezer, and forced herself to take a shower. The ice-cold water was the only relief she could find from the heat. When standing became too difficult, too exhausting, she sat down in the tub, pulled her knees close her chest, her arms wrapped around her hamstrings, and let the water beat down over her head and shoulders.

The rest of the day got away from her, in a daze, fucked up. She took a few more pulls from the chilled vodka bottle and the light soon slipped numbly into darkness. Kate coasted along the eerily deserted streets to Studio City and parked her car in an eerily empty garage, the engine cutting with a shudder, and took the elevator to the building's lobby. The ceiling lights seemed to be malfunctioning, twitching and pale. There was no one at the front desk, just an empty chair facing a blank security monitor, long shadows climbing the walls. She took another elevator and got off, walked down a long, angled hallway until she found the room she was looking for. The door was unlocked.

A blade of light cut through the darkness, slicing along the small room's wood-laminate floor. She flicked on the light switch, sent the shadows into hiding. The room was nearly bare: a cheap couch pushed up against the wall and a flat screen on the wall. The window shades were pulled down. It took her a minute to figure out the TV, to discover the unmarked disc in the DVD player, find the right input channel. Once she got the film going, she sat on the couch.

The version she watched must not have been finished. There were no opening titles. The sound was poorly mixed. At first the images were hard for her to process: humps of shadows, windswept dunes, close-ups on row upon row of sharp teeth. Then there was time-lapse footage of the sun rising and setting, which dissolved to a wiry nude man alone in the desert, his skin darkened by the heat, his head wrapped in rags. The man fell to his knees, digging at the edges of a wide, flat stone, shredding the skin of his fingers, growling like an animal. He extracted a small yellow lizard, the little thing squirming frantically in his fingers, brought the lizard up to his mouth and bit off its head. A single spurt of dark blood lashed his unshaven face, the lizard's limbs still thrashing.

Cut to a Steadicam shot sweeping through the halls of a desert palace, sand and dust sloping in the corners of empty rooms, cracked walls, fractured pillars. The soundtrack was stuffed with the sounds of wind, sucking sounds. There was the sudden image of a massive cave filled with sleeping bats. Then, back in the palace, there were people everywhere, dressed in fine silks and linens, wearing gold, gem-encrusted masks. Scores of elegant, beautiful women lying motionless on long couches, their breasts exposed, draped over the extravagant furniture. The bats awoke, fluttering into the cave in a great choreographed swoop. Similarly, the camera swooped around the palace's ballroom, revolving around dozens of couples as they danced a waltz, first one direction, then the next, revolutions around revolutions. A dazzling, corkscrewing overhead shot showed the dancers moving along the black lines of a pattern painted on the floor—the sigil of the abyss that Shea wore around his neck, the ring crowned by a cross.

There, in the center of the ring, Kate saw a small black dot take form, nothing more than a pinprick. The dot seemed to contain depth, an inky blackness, not a dot at all, but rather a hole. She focused her attention on this hole. Once again the images dissolved, the image of a woman's face—Anastazie Lhotsky or Melody Carmichael or Bianca Rhoads, whatever her name might be, if it even mattered—appearing beneath the ballroom, beneath the sigil, the camera zooming in on the woman's face while the image of the ballroom floor, the sigil, continued to spin, revolving again and again until the two images aligned, until the black hole appeared at the center of the woman's eye. The image of the ballroom continued to fade as the hole grew larger, entering the woman's eye. The sound of the wind returned—the noise of air sucked through a tube, a great pressure released. Soon, the hole was as large as half the screen, the entire screen, larger still—Kate covered her eyes, afraid of what she might see—until she felt the creeping dark come over her, sucking her inside, swallowing whole the room itself, warm as a mouth.

Then she was sliding down a sludge-slicked crevasse. She tumbled over herself a few times before turning over onto her back, pummeled by the uneven stone surface. Her clothes were torn open, skin bruised, shredded. Her legs were thrown over her head, and Kate fell far enough that she had time to draw a deep breath, to feel her heart in her throat, terrifyingly weightless. She was just about to scream again when she slapped the water's surface, hard as cement. Her body plunged deep down. There was nothing beyond the black silence, all-encompassing. She thought she was dead, felt the relief of that, and let her body go limp, turned over, her arms and legs hanging slack.

She surfaced. The smell around her was putrid, the smell of rot and ruin. The water was disgustingly warm, its taste foul. Wherever she was, it was dark; a single source of light shined through some deep, faraway crag, illuminating the swelling surface of some kind of underground lake. As far as she could see, the lake's rolling waves rippled with the misting rain. She was surrounded by bodies floating face down, uncared for, unloved, everyone left to dissolve in this godforsaken place. She saw men and women, old and young. She saw a clump of tangled babies, severed limbs, unidentifiable rafts of tissue and viscera.

The fetid water rolled over her, submerging her once again, choking her. The waves tossed her around like a ragdoll. Kate washed up onto some kind of shore, oil sands globbing onto her skin. She swiped away the muck from her eyes, crying out, vomiting brown fluid, emptying her stomach. She soldier-crawled to safety, her legs heavy and limp, waves slamming against her, threatening to pull her back in.

Then it was like she was watching a version of herself, leaving a version of herself behind, someone she no longer recognized. She watched the whole thing unfold like it was a camera shot—bird's eye view, spiraling upward—a scene in a movie that revealed Kate as she rolled onto her back. And as the camera pulled back, it revealed what could only be described as a mountain of flesh, a writhing pile of corpses, crushed together, arms and legs wriggling as a mass. Cries of agony echoed in the darkness. Kate saw this place now for what it was: a crack in the earth at the bottom of a deep ravine. In the distance, she caught a glimpse of giant creatures lumbering in the muck, things beyond comprehension, masses of humps and horns and innumerable limbs, feeding on the dead. And there, floating above everything, she saw Leonard Shea, knowing instinctively it was him, the keeper of the abyss—its overseer—Abaddon, the Angel of Death. His leathery black wings beat the air. This was his vision. Everything Kate had been given to see—the world below, her suffering—all of it belonged to him.

* * *

Kate stopped leaving her bungalow. She drank too much. She got fired from Clued-In-LA because she stopped responding to her editor's emails, stopped checking her voicemails. She ran out of money, both of her cards maxed out, rent past due. The cops sent two officers to check on her—banging on her front door, peeking through her windows—but she hid in the bathtub until they left.

She was obsessed with the story. The only thing that mattered was getting the story out there. People had to know what she'd seen. Suki assured Kate that they were still going to run it. The magazine said the second half of Kate's payment was on its way, but the money never showed and the story never ran. Suki said the delay was because Shea hadn't finished his film—there was no release date. They couldn't run the story without a release date. Then Suki stopped responding to Kate's emails, stopped answering her phone, her voicemail filled up. Her number was disconnected. Suki's social media accounts were deleted, as if she'd been swallowed up.

That's when Kate got scared. She worried she might be next. She knew too much. Still, she had to do something. She started a blog and posted the story there, fully aware of how crazy it sounded. The next day she received a cease and desist, certified mail, citing the contract she'd signed with the glossy. It was signed by the legal team of the company who owned the magazine. Her heart sank when she realized it was the same company that owned Shea's studio. And that's when Kate realized, all too late, that the magazine had never intended to run the story on Shea. The whole thing had been a catch and kill.

Kate needed to get out of LA. She grabbed her laptop, her phone, filled a duffel bag with her filthy clothes, and scraped together as much money as she could for gas and food. She threw everything in the backseat of her Honda and got behind the wheel. The engine choked and coughed. She beat the steering wheel with her fists and screamed. She pumped the gas pedal. The engine caught. She felt euphoric, laughing like a crazy person, swinging her car out into traffic and hitting the highway, heading back east, where people knew who she was.

Once she reached the desert the *engine hot* light popped on. Smoke started pouring out from under the hood. Her car started to slow. She pulled over onto the side of the highway, put on her flashers, screaming that this couldn't be happening—no, not now. The other cars kept driving by, a rush of sound and wind. Nobody seemed to notice her there, broken down on the side of the highway. No one seemed to care.

Blue and red police lights spun in her rearview mirror. Kate was crying now. The cop came to her window, motioned for her to lower it. He bent down, hands on his knees, and smiled, flashing small and sharp teeth like a piranha. She noticed the thin white scar that ran straight back over the curve of his shaved head, the chunk of flesh missing from his earlobe. His eyes were hidden behind mirror shades.

"License and registration," he said.

Kate was defiant. "If you try to take me anywhere, I'll scream."

He leaned forward, no longer smiling. "How much have you had to drink today?"

In that moment Kate knew she'd lost. He had all the power—the control. She watched as the cars continued passing her by on the highway, all their different colors, gleaming impossibly bright beneath the white desert sun.

"Open the door and exit the vehicle, Miss Murphy."

Kate always did have a knack for the story. She even knew how this one would end. She knew it would be just as bad as she feared because this was the real world. Bad things happened all the time—as bad as you could imagine. Soon, she would be a lost and lonely girl just like all the other lost and lonely girls, swallowed up and discarded. And she knew that no one would come searching for her. Only too late did Kate realize her worst fear—and for this she ached more deeply than she thought possible—that no one would come looking for her because no one would notice she was gone.

DEAD BABIES

THE NARROW CHURCH STEEPLE ascended beyond the early morning mists. Everything else he remembered was gone—buildings knocked down, roads torn up. Only the church remained, as distant and grim as always.

Things up close were always changing, replaced by new things. Faraway things, though, old things, those always stayed the same.

He couldn't get out of his own skin, despite the ugly revulsion, the constant shrill of anxious static. What was the self for if not easy and unearned forgiveness? So he returned to himself as a person haunted by nightmare returns to the light, out of necessity, an incessant nagging that reality in its very inescapability was the true horror.

* * *

The girl rang the brass bell, announced last call like an animal lowing. His better thinking blotted, sopped in the dregs of smoked black stout. The greasy lights twitched alive. A noxious cloud of cigarette smoke stalked the stained ceiling. A handful of repulsive old men in clothing the color of blotched and bruised skin skittered through the exit, locked in an anthem. He watched her closely, this bell ringer. She reminded him of his first wife—young, pretty, a vacuous form of flesh. She looked smart in her white sweater and dark square neck scarf. Her hair was cut short like a boy's. He liked that. He liked her smile. He told her as much when she came round to take his order, palming a sweaty bill her way—and would she mind accompanying him for a ride?

She met him out back in the alley in the low light, the shape of her utterly lost in an ugly brown coat and rubber boots. He held the passenger door open for her but she slyly circled around the front of the car, slender painted fingers gliding along the molded contours of the bonnet.

"This is a Spitfire," she said, tight jawed, grinding a gristle of gum with her molars. "A Mark III—you can tell by the weld lines on top of the wings." She stood exposed in the white light of the headlamps, her skin a heated flush of pink. "I know all about cars. My brother taught me. You know what he says about this one? He says they named this one for me."

* * *

He guided the machine along the village's winding roads, imagining it as some languid predatory beast, swooping through the night, dropping down from third to second when he took tight turns. Waves of small brown buildings emerged in the yellow light before receding from view, and the dusty glow of streaked reds and yellows held the fogged impression of memory. He thought of the machine as something subservient, something he could abuse—strangle the steering, choke it with gas. The engine whined. The low stone walls of town buckled and gave way to the haunted forms of trees, the stitched wooden fences of sleepy farmland.

He felt the weight of her hand draped over his thigh. She turned in her seat to better drink him in. "You're not from around here—that accent of yours." He met her green eyes in the rearview mirror as he hit a straightaway, dropped it into fourth.

* * *

He kept a bottle of Schnapps hidden away just for nights like this, something sweet he knew women didn't hate the taste of, something his first wife had liked when she was younger, and the two of them, him and this bell ringer, this girl, they passed it back and forth, nipping politely. When she'd had enough, she unceremoniously climbed on top of him and hiked her skirt up around her thighs. He undid his belt as she maneuvered weirdly out of her underwear. Then she ran her tongue over the salty spread of her palm—shaking now, nearly unnoticed—glistening the skin from her wrist to the tips of her fingers. In the cramped interior of his car he thought only of his first wife, ran her name through his mind, the disparate features of what he imagined added up to a face, her face, choosing to believe that the smell of the Schnapps was on her breath, something he could no longer recall as distinct, anyone's face now, not even a memory, or something connected to a memory, an image of teeth, the fleeting sensation of hair draped over skin. When it was over the girl rolled off him and back into the passenger seat, shifted her hips slightly as she pulled up her underwear. She smoothed her skirt over her thighs and lit a cigarette, staring out the window at nothing at all, or so he imagined.

* * *

The colors of the dark relaxed into a warm wrap of orange that haloed the horizon. He tweaked the radio's tuning knob between two fingers, slinking up and down the dial, unspooling wrecks of static, stern and disembodied voices. The girl finished off the Schnapps, no longer offering to share, comfortable enough to revel in her true self. He suggested they go for a walk, and she was either drunk enough or bored enough or dumb enough to find the idea enticing.

The crisp air smelled of mud and the sea. Mists rolled over the damp and rutted field like a miasma, harboring a metallic stink. The world did its best to hide from view, submerged in layers of gray. Soon they reached four perfectly intact chimneys some distance apart—brick badly scorched—separated by a flat bed of concrete, a filled-in foundation, its complex network of inky fractures spiked with stubborn brown weeds.

"I grew up two towns over, you know," the girl said. "Heard stories about this place all my life, what it used to be. Kids dropped off by teenage mothers in the middle of the night. They tore it all down after they found the babies—those little bundles of bones."

By then of course he was fully immersed in the rush of the city, busying himself with the delicate tread of living, the utter churn of it—happily married, blending in, ordering meals without reading the menu, always the same dish as the next table over. Then came the day when he read the blocky headlines that made it all come up poisonous black and bitter, when that lurking fear oozed into view. Mass graves found in disused sewers at Our Lady of Mercy, they said. Skeletal remains of thirty children discovered at orphanage.

His hands had shaken so violently that morning he'd spilled milk all over the table, a skin-staining mess of running ink and pulped paper.

The girl came in close, studying his face as if it held a dirty secret. "What's to get ugly about?" she said, somewhere between cruel mockery and irritated awe. "They were children of the devil." She turned and stomped away in those clunky rubber boots, belted her words into the still gray air. "Why you brought me out here to the middle of nowhere I'll never know." Then she extended her arms above her head, tumbled forward, and kicked her legs up in a cartwheel, her skirt rising and falling, giving a glimpse of pale skin. She righted herself, turned in dizzy circles—arms out at her sides—drunk on the open space.

He placed a hand on the nearest chimney, this brittle remnant of a thing swept away and so easily forgotten, and was startled to see dozens of peppered moths, their textured wings nearly imperceptible against the ashen brick, hiding in plain sight.

* * *

Two rows of carefully planted ash trees—their branches stripped by the cold—lined the path to the cathedral's entryway. An impressive coat of arms had been etched into the ancient stone above the wooden doors.

He tried the door but it was locked. He sat on the steps and he remembered the way the other children in the nice clothes used to taunt him, their sing-song voices calling him *home baby*. He remembered bloodying their mouths, the discolored crenulations of teeth in his throbbing knuckles. He remembered following the dark and imposing shapes of the sisters as they marched single file up the middle of the road, like in a ritual in a nightmare, returning to Our Lady of Mercy from primary school.

He'd been one of the lucky ones, strong enough and smart enough to take what he needed from those who were weak and stupid. He learned to hate the way they made him feel. And this was the truth he hoped most to slither out from under. He'd eaten his own. He'd liked the taste. He'd grown bigger on the blood and bones of the defenseless.

A priest stood over him, bent slightly with his hands on his knees, a look of righteous concern crossing his clean face. The priest was young, good looking, hair neatly combed.

Over the priest's shoulder he was loath to see that the sun had risen, that the sky had cleared. The white light cleaved heat through his skull—feeling scraped, raw—the initial harrowing blasts of a butchering hangover.

"Did you hear me?" the priest asked, putting a bird-light hand on his shoulder. "Services start soon. You can come in and rest up and listen or you can be on your way. But you can't sleep here."

* * *

A chunk of stone sat proudly in the center of the Spitfire's wrecked bonnet. The windscreen was webbed with deep fractures. All that was left of the driver's side window was a sugary dusting of glass shards on the black leather seat. He swept everything clean.

He stayed in low gear, kept the radio off, leaned forward in his seat at what felt like an extreme angle. The smell of alcohol seeped from his pores. The lines of the world looked disfigured, as if things had been dipped in acid and neglected, allowed to reform as something altogether strange, something frightening.

And there on one of those endless and identical backcountry roads, he came up looming behind a family as they strolled along in their Sunday best. They walked single file, country people: father leading the way, his wife and three children in tow.

Though he couldn't be sure, he thought he saw the girl there among them, the look on her pretty face—so much younger than he remembered. He betrayed his own feelings then, shrinking smaller in his rearview mirror before disappearing altogether, lost to a turn in the road, and then another, another. And when he was far enough away he pulled over, flung open the door, and released a black and bilious form until there was nothing left inside.

KING OF THE RATS

HE TALKED INCESSANTLY OF Transylvania, lording over a family of wolves, drinking the blood of virgins. Luke Temple—the only teenager in town who had access to a shotgun. When he answered the phone, his voice was washed over by the convulsions of death metal, static on the line.

"Okay," he said, "but afterward, you buy me a six-pack and some Camels."

For nearly an hour after I'd hung up, I sat staring at a blank television screen, my reflection warped in the curved glass. I was the kind of stoner who'd get stuck on the survival of spiders. And the next night, using Luke Temple's father's shotgun, I would slaughter a cow.

* * *

How is it that the bubonic plague was ever stopped from killing all of mankind? How is it that it hasn't returned, a thousand times over, to finish what it began?

* * *

Up close, the cow looked less sturdy than I'd imagined, skin tarped over steep hip bones. Blackness had taken a bite out of the moon, a half-eaten peanut butter cup. Luke shucked a shell into the shotgun's chamber. "I only grabbed one," he said. "You'll only need the one, right?"

I knew all about how guns worked from watching videos on the internet, how to hold them, what their various parts were.

Steam vapored into the night air from the lumpy frostbitten ground, cartoon souls in the moonlight, varnished and grim. The cow smelled like wet grass, big black eyes like television screens. There was a sudden awareness of need, an intense hunger curled fetus-like in my stomach. The word *plumbing* flashed through my mind as I squeezed the trigger and bruised the fuck out of my shoulder.

I heard Luke's voice ringing like from a distance—couldn't unwind the churn of his words—and only then realized that we were back in his car and driving. My hands were the bloodiest they'd been since birth.

That night, I wrote in a chat room online: "It's something I know I'm capable of now."

* * *

Eventually I defected to some shadowy cluster of braindead horror-film fanatics. We slurped warm foam out of Hamm's cans and hot-boxed Luke's backyard treehouse until our hair grew long and our grades slid low enough to justify dropping out.

I took up with the manager of a back-road video store, flabby Confederate sympathizer prone to histrionics, single mother of a dope-eyed infant with skin like third-hand smoke. She taught me the benefits of needling speed between my toes, how to bloom a woman's asshole without causing too much discomfort. "It's safer this way," she said. "No more kids this way."

From there, the familiar lull and weight of what I began to call the blackness—cancer of the mind.

She booted me from her double-wide when she found a thumbtack pinched in the firm sole of the baby's foot. I got caught up in my lie when I forgot that the thing couldn't walk upright yet.

* * *

Later that year, when winter was slushed up on the side of the roads, Luke Temple used his dad's shotgun to paint the walls of his bedroom. I'd long forgotten the shape of his teeth. No one wasted time on a wake.

* * *

It doesn't matter where I go or what I do or who I do it to. On the Greyhound bus at night, crossing fields of stunted, crooked trees, I can smile across the aisle at a girl and know terrible things she'll never know—not unless she's taught.

I'll do any odd job a man could dream up. And see it on through to the end.

STRANGE SIGNALS FROM THE CENTER OF THE EARTH

WE FIRST FOUND IT and thought nothing of it—this thick black cable, running up from a hole in the ground, wrapped several times around a scorched pylon, then split into many other cables—something innocuous like shapeless insects not known for their venom.

The cable, we learned, had been fed into each of the windows on our building's south side, facing the distant and cloudy city's center. It didn't seem to be attached to any of the companies whose logos inked the sleek envelopes we found in our mailboxes each month, and no extra cost was added to the expected—and already tolerated—expenses of living. So no one questioned what it might be, or what strange signal it might be carrying.

I noticed it one morning, snaking in between the frame of my warped window, pouring over its sagging wooden ledge. It was bolted fast to the wall with industrial strength staples, tracked downward and along the floor. I traced its length with my finger, hunched over. There was no end to it—at least, not that I could find. Instead, it ran the perimeter of my living space in some sort of ingenious circuit.

Back at the beginning, at the window, I would start again, always with my finger on the cable, never losing touch. And again, following its infinite looping around every wall of the apartment, I'd arrive back at the beginning, back at the old window, having somehow completed the circuit, yet never reaching any termination, any connection. The cable seemed to feed into nothing, except perhaps itself.

Each of my neighbors, I soon learned—in the units to my sides, above, and below—also had cables bolted along the floor moldings in their apartments, all leading to a splicer mounted on a nearby telephone pole. From there we followed its blackened length beyond our courtyard, and were led to a hole in the sidewalk some two blocks over. It was wide and deep, filled with an almost liquid blackness, smelling faintly of ash. It seemed harmless enough, this hole, though the roughness of its edges, flaking like chipped shale, and its network of clogged cracks bolting outward, toward the street, should, in retrospect, have signaled some alarm.

But the cost of living stayed static all the same. And so we, my neighbors and I, were content to keep on living as we always have, our convenient circuit of days and nights uninterrupted.

* * *

A few days passed. During the night hours, I began hearing dirges of interminable length, as if pounded out on a cheap organ, shrill and atonal. At first, this terrible music wormed its way through my head, intrusive like exploring tentacles, but I gradually grew to appreciate its horrible drone. Within a week, I was sleeping soundly through the night, lulled into vast, alien dreamscapes whose intricate webs of light and hatching splendor I would have never previously imagined possible.

After that, I stopped hearing the music all together, merely felt a gentle pulsing in my chest, as if the melody had curled into itself, dormant, leaving only a slightly percussive rhythm behind—something I imagined similar to the invisible touch of ghosts, a memory of a heartbeat.

* * *

I awoke and felt in my bones that I had been asleep for ages, the dull taste of dust gunking my mouth.

Where once there had been a single black cable looping my apartment, there were now three, cinched tight every few feet by black plastic quick ties, their ends neatly clipped. Yet the horror of this discovery quickly abated, paling when I saw that my old and warped window had been replaced by a crinkly metal duct, its surface unpolished and chalky, as wide and uninviting as a dank basement crawlspace, shuttling stale air into, or from, hitherto unknown depths. I recognized the faint smell of ash, that molten smell of the hole in the street, surprised by the dulling comfort of its familiarity.

I locked myself in the bathroom, tried to pry open the slit of a window behind the toilet tank, gummed shut with opaque, gray glue. Tiptoe on the lip of the tub, I was able to angle my head against the glass and see outside.

Unmarked vans, painted white with obsidian windows, lined the block unbroken, engines idling a quiet hum. A canopy of wires from the scorched pylons hung low over the street, attached to telescoping metal rods bolted to each of the strange vans' roofs, the sound of bulky generators sparking, crackling with radio static. The neighborhood was unrecognizable—having seemingly developed overnight into a complex of buzzing transformers—a confusion of wiring and raw, unharnessed electricity, the offensive stink of chemical smoke.

There were no children playing in the street. There was no traffic. No sky. No natural light. No recognizable life.

I did not sleep well that night, too scared to leave my apartment. Every time I felt the lull and settle of my heartbeat, I'd imagine such frightful sounds, the sounds of the duct's plating popping, flexing, as if someone or something were attempting to climb up from its black void.

* * *

There were my neighbors—from the units to my sides, above, and below me—there in the center of some strange cobblestone square, heads pulled back, chins jutting toward the face of the ancient astronomical clock, its seven gnarly arms askew, monitoring a system of time far beyond our understanding, far older than the revolutions of the sun, the tides of our tired ocean.

Smell of ash. A mist rolled through the air, obscuring the surrounding village.

The clock's hands locked into place with an aching turning of hidden gears, and the lurching of its bell sounded through the stilted air, an irregular, otherworldly rhythm, wet like the chops of a butcher's cleaver against his block. My neighbors—I stood directly behind them now—they turned to me, heads lolling, and I saw that their eyes had gone black, obsidian like ashen, polished stones.

* * *

I went up and down the fourth-floor hallway, knocking on doors, ringing buzzers. Nothing. Looking over the railing of the staircase, I saw the bottom half of the building submerged in what looked like scorched oil, rippling with brilliant kaleidoscopic fireworks, rainbows of iridescent light.

The smell was overpowering.

* * *

In my dreams, my building has sunk deep into the Earth's crust, as if our entire neighborhood had been carved in stone, just one of many unfathomably large chambers filled with still night air, what were once bubbled-up air pockets carried to the surface by rapidly cooling molten sludge.

The cables from our pylons descend from beyond our vision, from the blackness above, wrapped around our arms, our waists, our necks, gracefully lifting and dropping us through the air like so many marionettes. Our movements are a ballet, beautiful and without the slightest hint of human error. Such careful choreography cannot possibly be described, and every passing moment is utterly blissful in its weightlessness.

Our lives are now set to soundless music, scored by the scorched rhythms of blood flow, the Earth's pulse. Yawning chasms open beneath us, the echo of the void radiating, rising up from untold depths, a wall of ripped sound from ancient engines. Everything spins like a wondrous carousel, a perpetual motion machine comprised of pulleys and levers beyond human engineering.

Electricity flows through our veins, our muscles nothing more than conduits, and our eyes glow orange and fierce in the darkness. From below, it would be easy to mistake our glorious airborne dance for a star-filled sky furious with motion, a vision of time flashing forward, the universe overflowing, stretching into a steady stream of new light.

* * *

One by one, throughout the building you hear them, televisions, flipping on with a hollow ringing tone. The signal received.

A flowing of molten rock, pouring outward in the direction of my living room, yet dipping down just below the curved glass of the TV screen. Patterns of light. A low gurgle of static sounding like so much beastly noise, or wind, the rattle of chalky bones.

Something is lost in between, between two crags of stone, some decipherable ray of light.

The screen is smeared like an oil-obscured mirror, and I have spent so much time staring at its blackened surface, fascinated by the strange hovering shapes looming over my reflection's shoulders, long, gnarled fingers of some terrible monster—a projection of my fears constantly blooming in the darkness of an empty, windowless room.

EYES IN THE DUST

CORTLAND STILL BLAMED HIMSELF for Claire's death. It was difficult not to. After all, he'd spent an entire weekend badgering her to come with him. He'd needed someone to help him carry everything necessary to study the region's topography. The fate of his thesis, the term—and therefore his entire scholarship—was at stake. She was right, of course, that the recent hurricane off the coast of Maine had brought on some two or three months of rain in just under a week, a thousand-year storm. The usual footpaths that led up into the hills around Mountain Top Lake would be washed out, the rocks slick, perilous. But he hadn't listened.

For her last day on Earth, Claire chose to wear a bright yellow raincoat with matching rubber boots. They didn't have the best grip but they would keep her feet dry. The last thing she wanted, she said, was to spend the entire day with wet socks.

Things started off badly. An entire hour was swallowed by the damp, dark morning when Cortland's Jeep got lodged in the muddy, backwoods roads. By the time they began hiking the trail at the base of Eagle Bluff, the sky was a restlessly churning vortex of gilded silver—a series of torrential downpours giving way to oddly beautiful sun-showers. In his bulky pack, Cortland carried the majority of the equipment, his self-leveling surveying instrument, its massive tripod, various binoculars, maps, and GPS devices, while Claire carried the food and water, a high-powered strobe, and heat packs. There was no way he was coming back down without the data he needed to finish his research paper on Maine's glacial moraines.

The first bad omen—in retrospect, so many things looked like bad omens—occurred about halfway up the trail: the rubber treads of Claire's rain boots couldn't get a good grip on the mossy granite and she scraped both of her palms in an attempt to break a particularly nasty fall. "This is stupid," she said, her jawline clenched as she pushed herself back onto her feet. "We shouldn't be up here and you know it." Again, she was right. Trekking up the bluff face, miles away from help, was more than stupid—it was irresponsible. He regretted nothing more than not coming to her side at that moment, holding her in his arms and telling her that he was wrong to keep pushing on, that he was sorry, that they would go home, build a fire, dry up, and get warm. But he hadn't done any of that. Instead, he doubled down on his stubbornness. "Are you done throwing your fit?" he said, ignoring the look on her face as she seethed. Now, whenever Cortland thought of her, it was that face he remembered, that awful look of anger and hurt. He couldn't get it out of his head.

There was no way Cortland could have known that those would be some of the last words he ever spoke to her, Claire, the woman he was engaged to marry, the love of his life. There was no way he could have known. And so he'd carried on, leading the way into that disastrous afternoon, the events of which would forever haunt his remaining days.

* * *

Even by the impossible standards of global corporations, Applied Logistics was a behemoth, with more than a hundred offices spread throughout nearly forty countries, including all of the world's major economic superpowers. They had their tentacles firmly threaded through everything: financial services, oil, pharmaceuticals. Whatever the industry, as long as it generated cash, some modicum of economic and political influence, Applied Logistics, or the Firm, as they liked to be called, had a team of consultants hoteling somewhere nearby, doling out invaluable advice via conference calls and meticulously researched reports. In the few years since Cortland had finished successfully defending his dissertation—years wasted unhappily as an adjunct professor for various community colleges in small, seemingly interchangeable cities—he'd never had any dealings with the Firm. And so it came as quite a surprise when he answered a call from a headhunter with a lucrative assignment: two months in an undisclosed remote area studying what was presumed to be an impact crater unearthed after the collapse of a cave network, with guaranteed future consultations on the land's mining operations.

This was just the kind of lucky break he'd been dying for. Claire would have scoffed at the notion of being a wonk, writing research at the behest of corporate interests, but this offer that was too good to refuse. There was no reason not to accept.

A few days after he'd worked out the paperwork with the headhunter, Cortland sat alone in the luxurious cabin of an Applied Logistics jet. Even for a big-money corporate job, the whole thing was abnormally secretive. They took off from a private airstrip outside DC, after waiting hours for an expected and heavy fog to roll in. Both of his cell phones were confiscated before takeoff—he was told they'd be returned to him the following morning—apparently as a security precaution. Whoever was calling the shots didn't want Cortland to know where he was going.

Perhaps half a day later they landed in some nameless gray zone in some nameless gray country. Grim-faced soldiers stood motionless along the chain-link fence at the far end of the landing strip. Was he in Poland? He studied their uniforms, made a mental note to look them up later, but forgot about it as soon as a man in a black coat and sunglasses led him to a seaplane inside a massive hanger. They were taking off in five minutes, the man said.

Again, hours passed. Cortland fell asleep, woke to a smooth landing. The seaplane taxied leisurely before coming to a complete stop, waters rocking it gently. Behind the cockpit door, Cortland discerned the hiss of walkie talkies. Moments later, he was escorted to a small boat equipped with an outboard motor. The driver was dressed in a black wetsuit, black life vest, his face obscured by a balaclava. They did not exchange greetings. Cortland was taken swiftly to the shoreline. It was blackest night and the stars were blindingly bright. There was only a moment to notice the rippled reflection of the moon on the dark oily water, the dense, bristled outline of evergreens atop what appeared to be massive stone formations surrounding the lake, or quarry, whatever it was. The sound of the outboard motor was deafening, limitless, echoing back upon itself in a rolling wave.

The belly of the boat ground harshly onto a stony beach. Two men in blue-shirt uniforms—the distinctive Applied Logistics logo emblazoned on their chests—helped Cortland onto land. The boat's driver pushed off and retreated into the night. No time to waste. The sound of the outboard was smaller, softer, now just a whine in the distance. Maglites in hand, the two blue-shirts guided Cortland up a winding trail to his cabin, ascending wide spiral risers, talking all the while in heavily accented English, something vague and indiscernibly Eastern European, not allowing him time to think, informing him that although he had no electricity or standardized plumbing, he had gas lamps and a generator-powered water pump, an outhouse, a wood-burning stove, a well-stocked library to help pass the time, that he would have plenty of time in addition to all of the basic amenities, all the food he could ever wish to eat, whatever else it was he had requested on the account's charge code. In the morning, they said, his questions would be answered. He had a meeting scheduled with Mr. Robinson, "the principal" they called him. Until then, he'd need to get some sleep. He had a long day ahead of him, lots of work. And then Cortland stood just beyond the threshold of the small cabin, alone, the door clicking shut softly behind him.

His bags had been placed neatly along the wall, cell phones—worthless hunks of plastic without electricity to charge them—placed neatly on the kitchen table. The copper-lined gas lamps pulsed serenely on the wall, giving the cabin a coziness that Cortland found intoxicating. Exhausted, his mind spinning with questions, he kicked off his boots, crossed the room with a few long strides, and crashed into the twin bed.

As he fell asleep, he registered a distant humming and wondered, perhaps, if it was some sort of machine working through the night, a rock drill, or perhaps a large generator. It was just a fleeting thought, however, because sleep soon overtook him, submerging him in its warm black flow.

* * *

The morning filled the interior of the cabin with radiant sunlight. Cortland fried eggs in a perfectly seasoned cast-iron skillet, brewed luxuriously dark coffee in a glass percolator. He opened a small window over the stainless-steel kitchen sink and immediately the smell of pine was everywhere. Again, that odd buzzing noise droned in the distance. It definitely wasn't a machine, he realized. It almost sounded like crickets, but much louder, maybe even cicadas, with barely perceptible undercurrents of—as ridiculous as it might sound—a joyous melody.

Cortland guessed he was somewhere in Siberia, perhaps the Taiga, quite a ways from home, from anywhere, really. Birds called in the distance. The air was thick with humidity and was actually quite sweltering. No wind seemed to penetrate the deep forest. After eating his food, he took a few moments to look through the bookcases on the far side of the room, and was surprised to find a carefully curated collection of philosophy, which included numerous works by Spinoza and Leibniz, two of Cortland's major influences. Even more surprising, however, was finding a dog-eared paperback of his dissertation—a slim and nervous book—sandwiched between two much larger, leather-bound books. He pulled the book from the shelf and held it in two hands. *The Nonhuman Turn: Cognition, Decision Making, and Will in Everyday Objects.* Cortland opened the book and flipped through a few pages. Whoever had read through this particular copy had underlined dozens of passages, made copious notes in the margins in handwriting that was largely indecipherable. He returned the book to the shelf. Sure, it had been published by a widely respected university press, but it had gone nowhere, hadn't even secured him a job. He'd been warned that panpsychism would never be taken seriously by academia. An advisor actually took him aside one day and told him that abandoning his empirical studies in geology for such nonsense would be career suicide. But he hadn't wanted anything to do with reality after Claire had passed. He knew that his understanding, his intuiting, of the natural world was far more complex than the naysayers could ever fathom. In the end, it hadn't mattered. His book barely sold fifty copies and was quickly forgotten. The field continued to evolve without him, always new theories gaining traction, supplying the footnotes for even newer theories.

Dishes soaking in the sink, he packed a leather satchel with a notebook, some binoculars, and a voice recorder that was issued by the Firm. Out of habit, Cortland took one last look at his personal cell phone. Still no signal. Then he was out the door.

His cabin sat atop a wide, round hill. In the distance, through a pocket of trees, he could see the roofs of perhaps half a dozen cottages, all of them either asphalt shingle or tin. Already sweating from the heat, he made his way down the footpath. He saw now in the daylight that it was the massive roots of surrounding trees that acted as the risers he'd climbed the night before, as elegant and idyllic as any planned public space in any city he'd ever traveled to.

At the entrance to the village, indicated by a crude archway constructed by two birches, a dark-haired boy wearing khaki shorts and an oversized, hand-me-down T-shirt greeted Cortland with a wave. He appeared to be a native, perhaps one of the Ket people Cortland remembered reading about in an undergrad sociology class. The boy was barefoot, Cortland noticed, his feet scabby with filth. "You are Mr. Cortland?" he said in shockingly good English. Cortland nodded. "Please follow me. I will take you to the principal. He is expecting you."

Together they walked, the boy moving swiftly and Cortland doing his best to keep up while taking in the surroundings. In the distance, sunlight rippled gold on the surface of the water through the trees. The cabins were interspersed somewhat irregularly. Dirt footpaths, swept clean of pine needles, had been lined with tree branches. All of the structures were expertly built, composed of new and expensive materials. They passed through the center of the village, where outdoor cupboards had been built high up in a cluster of trees, their trunks wrapped with sheet metal, no doubt to dissuade bears from finding an easy meal. From there, the path forked, the right side leading into the woods, the left toward yet another tree-root staircase, this one spiraling down toward the stony beach. "Mr. Robinson is there," the boy said, gesturing to a cabin.

"This is a very nice village you have here," Cortland said. "Are you from the area?" And then, after it became clear that the boy wasn't going to answer, "What is your name?"

The boy's face was set. "I am told to teach you nothing," he said. "Mr. Robinson will teach you everything. Please go."

Before Cortland had a chance to respond, to ask another question, the door to the cabin swung open, revealing a short, round man in green fatigues. He wore silver-frame glasses and his eyes were small, ringed with dark circles. "Please come in," he said. "I expected you tomorrow. But there's nothing to be done for that now."

Inside, the cabin was a disaster. The kitchen looked as if it hadn't been cleaned in days. Dishes were stacked haphazardly in the sink and the stove was crusted with burned food. Thick black flies buzzed all over everything. The windows were closed, curtains pulled. The shut-in smell was overpowering. In the corner of the room, a shirtless man lay in bed. Big beads of sweat stippled his forehead, ran lines through the caked dust that darkened his face.

"He has a fever," Cortland said, taking a few decisive steps toward the bed. He saw the man's eyes flutter open and roll up into his head, all bloodshot whites. "Jesus, he must be burning up." Robinson, surprisingly quick, grabbed Cortland by the arm and held tight.

He spoke rapid fire. "Leave him. Please. It's nothing. An insect bite. He was working at the site earlier today and came down with it. Happens all the time here. I've already radioed in for a boat." When Robinson smiled, his teeth large, almost phosphorescent, Cortland got the feeling that it was meant to relax him. It did anything but. "There's no cause for alarm," Robinson said, his voice softer now, controlled. "I must apologize for the state of things around here. I've been at the site for weeks. Haven't had much time for cleaning. And as I said, I was expecting you tomorrow."

"He needs medical attention," Cortland said.

"I'm well aware of that, Mr. Cortland." Robinson pulled a chair from the kitchen table. "Have a seat. You're my guest here, so please make yourself comfortable." He nodded to the man on the bed. "He'll be taken care of in no time at all. You'll see." Again, that phosphorescent smile.

As if to punctuate his statement, the door opened and two men entered. They wore sunglasses and the same Applied Logistics uniforms as Cortland's chaperones from the night before. One of the men, a crooked scar twisting his upper lip, carried a folding stretcher under his arm and the other, his left hand bearing a gaudy gold ring, a first-aid kit. Cortland sat at the table and watched, utterly bewildered. Within minutes, the two men had loaded up their patient onto the stretcher, given him a shot of something that made his breathing noticeably slow, and taken him away. After seeing them out, Robinson took a seat at the table opposite Cortland.

"I do apologize for you having to see that," Robinson said. "I assure you it was merely bad timing. The forest belongs to the insects, you see. It's their kingdom. You should see the clouds of mosquitoes deep in the woods—an ungodly sight. Really something to behold. We are, for the time being, merely intruders in a vacuous world I'm afraid we don't understand. At least not yet." He laughed softly. His face went suddenly serious. "You must have a lot of questions."

Cortland got straight to business. His patience was running thin and he was tired of being kept in the dark. "Let's start with the work site you've referred to." He tossed his satchel onto the table, took out the voice recorder. "I'm told it was a collapsed cave network, but I'd like to hear it from you." He flipped on the recorder. "Tell me why I'm here."

Robinson took his time and explained in great detail. Just over a month ago, a collapse had indeed occurred in an area the locals referred to as Purgatory Gulch, a wide bed of rock that lay between two massive stone outcroppings. These two formations were colloquially known as Heaven and Hell, the former majestic in scale, abundant in plant life, the latter a desolate hunk of blackened rock, long rumored to be the stubborn melt from an impact crater. Apparently those rumors proved true, because the crater uncovered by the collapse was enormous. The fact that the two formations had emerged within a crater in the first place was something of a geological abnormality, a rare natural phenomenon known as "mountains in a moat." Cortland asked for specifics, the approximate year of the impact, the diameter of the crater, whether or not there was present a central peak uplift, any remnants of ejecta. "I'll need to review the field notes," he said. "Everything you've got." It was a reasonable enough request and Robinson agreed to have them delivered to Cortland's cottage, redacted as necessary of course, the following morning.

A few days after the crater had been discovered, Robinson continued, its bottom had fallen out, behaving rather like a sinkhole. This hole had initially been excavated by scouts employed by the Firm's oil and gas practice. Although no signs of oil were found, they did discover trace amounts of rich minerals used in the production of advanced electronics, such as smartphones. And so another practice, resources and minerals, for which Robinson served as the principal, had taken over. The minerals had proved difficult to extract, dangerous even. The hole was seemingly growing deeper by the day. Even the surrounding forest was a threat: new trails had been blazed, the village had been erected, equipment airlifted in. Perhaps a dozen satellite sites were erected around the perimeter of the crater and complex networks of tunnels were dug into the rock sheet in an effort to create easier access. Significant resources were expended. At first, the Firm had tried conventional mining operations. Natives were brought in, easily lured by promises of steady work, free meals, and limitless vodka. "For quite a while," Robinson said, "local labor was as abundant as it was cheap. But lately, we have had little luck persuading the men in the area to accept our offers. They believe something is amiss." He smirked. "Superstitious people that they are. Most have taken to steady drinking to pass the days. Though we have established something of a rapport with one of their elders, who acts as a liaison, tensions are still high. Relations are delicate."

"So why me?" Cortland said, exasperated. "Why bring me out here? I don't have any experience with extractions."

Again, Robinson laughed his soft laugh. "You're not here to oversee the mining operation—in fact, all of that has been put on hold indefinitely. The Firm is well informed of this. I write them daily reports on our progress here." He leaned forward, his eyes on the voice recorder. "You're here because of your academic work, plain and simple. What we have here is not something as mundane as a mineral deposit, but rather what I believe to be the basis for an entirely new industry. Imagine for a moment communicating over vast distances without the aid of cellular technology, tapping into the cloud without an internet connection, downloading entire systems of knowledge in an instant. Absurd, yes? Well, I believe that we have discovered a substance that can make all of that possible. Even more than that. The limit is merely our own imagination. Come, I will show you."

* * *

There stood Heaven and Hell, just as Robinson had described them, looming shadowy in the distance. And there, shrouded in the misty valley enveloping the two great stones, was the hole. The size of it was much larger than Cortland could have imagined, perhaps thirty to forty meters in radius. It had to have been several thousand million years old. Its shape was divine, a perfect circle—too perfect—with sheer walls of rock face that machines could not have bored more efficiently. He'd never seen a crater look like this before, so precise, so massive. Its blackened depths suddenly hatched a magnificent, amorphous cloud of bats. The leathery sound of their erratic flight quickly silenced as they disappeared into the immense sky.

"Magnificent, isn't it?" Robinson said, clearly aware of the grandeur of the sight. "Mind your step," he said as Cortland descended the stone-lined footpath. "The trail here can get quite slippery." There's no way Robinson could have meant anything by those words, but they stuck in Cortland's guts like daggers, instantly flooding his memory with visions of Claire, that day at Mountain Top Lake.

Still, he pushed on, pushed away the pain, the principal's voice fading behind him. Cortland followed the path as it arced around the site, slowly descending in elevation as he made his way around, a lazy spiral. Dozens of men—blue-shirts and nonuniformed locals alike—stood near the base of a massive steel scaffold, the size of a small, offshore oil rig, its primary structure scaling at least fifty feet high, elevated on cement pillars firmly embedded in the surrounding rock. The top of the scaffold housed a tower crane, as well as a complex system of jibs, winches, and dozens of tightly coiled steel lines. A few clustered men talked quietly among themselves, while others stood alone, stared contemplatively into the crater. As Cortland came close, his boots kicking up clouds of dust in the loose bed of sunbaked dirt spread atop the rock bed, the door to the operator's cockpit snapped open. A tall, wiry man emerged, swung round onto the step ladder, and slid down like a superhero in a comic book, his knees bending slightly on impact. "Mr. Cortland?" he said, betraying a heavy German accent. He stood straight and held out one of his large, gloved hands.

He was tall and wore tight, black clothing, as well as a light-mounted hardhat and climber's rig. His face was hidden behind a full, reddish-blond beard and aviator's glasses. Before Cortland could take his hand, the man quickly removed the glove. "Forgive me," he said. "My hand will be sweaty. We have been working all through the morning." Cortland took the man's hand and shook. He was remarkably strong and his forearm rippled with muscles.

"Preparing for anything?" Cortland asked.

"The platform installation along the chasm," the man said. "It will make unaided descent possible. Finally, after all this time, we can get our equipment down there."

Robinson shuffled up behind Cortland. "I see you've introduced yourself," he said to the German. Then, "Mr. Cortland, please meet our esteemed Mr. Heinrich—one of the world's foremost rock climbers."

"So they say," Heinrich said, smiling warmly at Cortland. "And you are going to tell us what it is we have down there." He turned slightly and nodded toward the hole.

"You mentioned equipment," Cortland said, impatience getting the best of him. "I'd like to hear how things have been going so far."

Robinson laughed a little too loudly. "Always cutting to the chase, aren't you? All of this will be discussed tonight, over dinner at my cabin. And much more, of course. It is far too sensitive a subject to discuss here." At this, Heinrich merely continued to smile, perhaps humoring Robinson, the reflective silver of his sunglasses glaring beneath the brutal white sun, offering Cortland only an image of himself, red faced and wide eyed. The idea of dining in Robinson's filthy cottage made Cortland's stomach turn. He thought of the bloated black flies, the shut-in smell, that look of anguish he'd seen upon the face of the man who had suffered the insect bite.

"If that is the case," Heinrich said, smearing at the sheen of sweat on his forehead with a dusty forearm, "you must excuse me. I need to head back up to the village and clean up."

Cortland spent the next hour walking the footpath that had been blazed around the perimeter of the hole, always careful to maintain a safe distance from its precipice, accompanied at all times by Robinson. The two men discussed Cortland's work in great detail, Robinson asking many questions, listening carefully. After they had completed the circle, standing once more beneath the tower crane, Cortland saw that the otherwise smooth rock face shattered into a thin, jagged seam. His eyes followed the gash as it widened into a black chasm, disappeared into the depths.

"This was created with strings of explosives," Robinson said, "as well as a pneumatic drill, to facilitate the construction of the platforms and their connective stairs. The walls of the hole are simply too sheer otherwise. Structural analysis has ensured that it is quite safe, really. The project will begin in earnest tomorrow." He turned and began making his way toward the path. "Follow me, please."

Cortland took a few steps, then, overcome by a sudden urge, turned and looked out once more upon the horizon. The darkened sun, now a fiery disc, slid behind the tree line, cast the entire valley in purple shadow. There, standing at the edge of the crater, in the sweltering forest heat, Cortland saw something that gave him chills: a woman in a yellow raincoat and matching rubber boots, her face blurry in the distance, a smudge of fleshy color, impossible to make out yet unmistakably Claire's. His hand, as if acting on its own, shot out in her direction, reaching toward her. And then she was gone, disappeared behind a wall of mist. Perhaps the heat was getting to him. Or perhaps he was still exhausted from traveling. Either way, it had been an illusion. It had to be. Cortland shook it off, caught up with Robinson, and followed him back up into the village.

* * *

Cortland was the last to arrive at Robinson's cottage that night, where, in addition to his host, he was greeted by Heinrich and an old man with dark eyes and dust-caked hair, presumably the native liaison Robinson had mentioned earlier. It was just after sundown, and Cortland was greatly relieved to find that the place had been tidied. Not just tidied, the cottage had been scrubbed spotless. The windows were open, screens fitted carefully in their empty frames. The floor was mopped and polished. A large mosquito net affixed to the ceiling draped over the wide dinner table, where the other men sat. Placed at the table's center was an ornate candelabra, its many arms fitted with rough chunks of blood-red wax. The oily flames provided the only source of light, cast long and crooked shadows that climbed the walls, made the thick netting glow like some kind of carnival tent.

"You remember Mr. Heinrich, of course," Robinson said, handing Cortland a glass of wine. "Malbec is okay? Good."

Robinson lifted the mosquito netting and gestured for Cortland to take a seat at the table. It was impossible to ignore the fact that Robinson—or Heinrich for that matter—had failed to introduce Cortland to the old man, but before he could do so himself, Heinrich sat down and began making conversation. He appeared rather loose from drinking. His sweat-slicked face gleamed in the candlelight.

Robinson soon joined them and the two men took turns asking Cortland about his flight in, his general impressions of the village, the amenities, whether or not he had yet encountered the mosquitos. No one mentioned the site, how they had gotten here, what they were doing here. And all the while, the old man opposite Cortland stared silently. It was unnerving, to say the least, but the talk at the table moved swiftly and, despite his initial uneasiness, Cortland found himself growing more animated, relaxing into the setting. Robinson did well at playing a good host; he laughed at everyone's jokes, made sure that Cortland's wine glass stayed full. Soon enough, the food arrived, wheeled in on trays by one of the natives.

"We sit here, now, on top of what was once one of the largest, most complex cave networks on the entire planet," Robinson said, ripping loose a chunk of bread with his teeth. He chewed for a moment, slowly rolling the food from one side of his mouth to the other, before continuing. "It is perhaps no coincidence that the forest that surrounds us also contains a veritable constellation of impact craters, some as old as the soil itself. These things are not a coincidence. One informs the other. The seams of life on this planet were ripped open abruptly, exposing the abyss from which all things crawled, and still others wisely stayed behind."

Cortland worried that he'd had too much to drink. The room seemed to swell and sigh with the flicker of the candlelight. The night had been easygoing and fun, but Robinson's tone now was somber, contemplative, a bit more than intense. Cortland looked to the old man across the table, still just sitting there silent, not eating, always watching.

"In the short time that Mr. Heinrich has been with us here," Robinson continued, "I have been unable to answer many of his questions about the site. I lack imagination, creativity. The truth of the matter is that the nature of our work here is unknown even to me."

Cortland rubbed his eyes, took another look at the table. Heinrich didn't so much look flushed with drink as he desperate and scared. Robinson's words seemed to highlight an undercurrent of paranoia, fear—but of what? It dawned on Cortland that they were isolated here, out in these woods, this forest, miles away from the outside world.

Robinson's grating smile collapsed for perhaps the first time that day, and in its place, a grave look that seemed to suck the air from the room. There followed an unbearable silence, broken only when Cortland again heard the humming in the distance, somewhere out there in all that black beyond the warmth of the candlelight, the safety of the mosquito netting. And hearing that sound again made him realize that it had always been there, that he had somehow tuned it out for the entire day, as if he were getting used to it, like white noise.

"Mankind long ago evacuated the notion of progress," Robinson said, "of evolution. Everything is twisted in time and space—you've written about this very thing, Mr. Cortland. The outside has become the inside. The great wheel will return man to the slime from which he emerged. This is what we really are. The slime molds of your studies exhibiting signs of rational intelligence. Our greatest intellectual pursuits so meaningless in the constant struggle for survival. Life, as we have come to understand it, is composed of nothing more than the elements of infinity, the darkness that corrupts all things."

"I don't know what you mean," Cortland said. "I don't know what any of this means. You're speaking in riddles." The candlelight played tricks with his vision. Robinson's eyes disappeared behind pools of shadow. "If you're referring to the ideas in my book, they're really rather simple. I think that you've misunderstood—"

"Things arrived from outside that are not us," Robinson said, interrupting, "and these things somehow survived millions of years beneath the surface of our planet. They are inorganic to us, and yet still alive. For these things, to decay is to build, to spread darkness is to enlighten. They eat by starving themselves, propagate their species by spreading death. They are the everlasting life that man has unceasingly sought—*being* without thought."

The old man abruptly stood up, his chair legs scraping against the floor. He gave Robinson a stern look before ducking down, disappearing beyond the mosquito net. Cortland again looked to Heinrich; he appeared to be listening to Robinson with the utmost attention, the indoctrinated taking in a sermon. Did he not think this was odd? Robinson's ravings were those of a madman.

The humming beyond the windows grew louder, millions of crickets chirping all at once, a solid wall of sound. It was as gorgeous as any symphony Cortland had ever heard, seemingly lulling him into some kind of foggy stupor.

Robinson turned his head slightly, brought a single finger to his lips, as if to hush anything Cortland might say, or perhaps his train of his thought. "Do you hear that? It's the sound of the fabric of all things. They are weaving a new beginning, a new reality." Cortland watched as Heinrich closed his eyes, lowered his head as if in prayer. "Imagine the Earth as it was in its earliest stages," Robinson said, "nothing more than a pupa, so many millions of years ago. From vast distances arrives a storm. Sentient stones—the only word our language has for these beings—the building blocks of life, of existence beyond reason, rain from the sky, bursting into flame. They scorch the ground, bury themselves deep beneath the surface of things, slumbering golems, all of them. Above, the ground crumbles back into place, incubating this new life. A life from beyond found not among the stars but beneath our very feet. It is here and it has awoken."

Cortland laughed. He couldn't help himself. "You can't be serious. If you're familiar with my work then you'd know that I write about very real things in a very real world, the slime molds you mentioned earlier, for instance, *Physarum polycephalum*. What you're talking about is absurd. Speculations. Science fiction."

His words seemed to break Robinson's spell. The principal laughed with him. "Of course it is. Totally absurd. But fun to think about nonetheless. No?" Heinrich joined in on the laughter. Suddenly the pleasant mood of the early evening was restored. Robinson poured Cortland another glass of wine. At this point he was close to polishing off two bottles, no wonder he'd sensed the mood souring—he was wasted. He must have misunderstood Robinson's little soliloquy. That's all it had been: a soliloquy. Talk returned to tall tales and optimism about the prospects of the site. Cortland didn't even notice that the humming had ceased. By the time he'd finished yet another glass of wine he was barely conscious of anything at all.

* * *

Even the moonlight couldn't penetrate the thick canopy of the forest. Cortland borrowed a flashlight from Robinson just to make his way back to his cottage, stumbled after the thin, pale beam as it swept over the twisted trail. He was very drunk. Yet somehow he made it back unharmed, crashed into bed, still wearing his clothes, and became lost in the darkness of the night. Even with his eyes wide open, he couldn't see an inch in front of his face. The night outside was filled with sharp and angular noises that took on a sinister dimension.

He breathed deeply. He was anxious. Somehow the alcohol had energized his system rather than tiring him. He took in great heaps of breath in hopes that it would calm him down, but only felt as if he were choking on the darkness, his mouth full of dust. The memory of Claire, the regret, coursed through his blood like a poison. He'd been out in the woods for only a day and already he was losing it. He laughed wildly at the thought.

There was always the work. He needed to focus on his work. In the morning he'd review the field notes for the original excavation. Something was off here—that much was obvious. Something wasn't right with the men at the site, the way they all stood around the crater, not talking, blinking. Something definitely wasn't right with Robinson. He'd been out in the woods too long, under too much pressure from the Firm perhaps.

Yes, in the morning, he'd review the field notes. That would help. Certainly that would help shine a light on all this madness.

* * *

He dreamed about that fateful afternoon at Mountain Top Lake, as he so often did, forever reliving the moments he could never forget.

The rain had mercifully ceased as they reached the top of Eagle Bluff, though the sky had remained silver, volatile. Cortland set up his equipment as Claire plopped down on one of the wide, flat rocks overlooking the moraine. The view was gorgeous: a steep decline over an outcropping, the vista of a grassy rock bed. A twenty-foot-tall wall of stratified glacial sand and gravel ran the length of one side of the rock bed, its layers a record of the passage of time as the ancient glacier had pushed through the land through sheer force of will.

A few moments later, they shared a lunch of dry tuna sandwiches and carrot sticks. Claire was still fuming over their spat and their conversation was terse, relegated to quick questions and monosyllabic responses. Cortland was too proud to apologize and besides, he knew she'd forgive him easily once they were back in town, laid out on the couch, comfortably eating hot pizza in front of an old black-and-white movie.

Cortland never did fully understand why he did what he did next. Maybe he was trying to get on her good side. Or maybe he just felt the need to say something, anything at all. "There are some bear caves around here," he said. "Up in the rocks over there." He pointed to a slope of granite chunks on the far side of the moraine. "Perfect time of year to check them out, while they're out foraging. You interested?" He asked this fully knowing that she would be. Claire loved any and all animals, loved studying their habitats, their tracks, even their droppings. She was good that way, respected life in all its many forms.

Splayed out on the rocks, her legs crossed beneath her in those big rubber boots, Claire took a hair tie out of her jacket pocket, pulled back her wet, shoulder-length hair into a tight ponytail. The clouds opened for just a moment, letting through a blaze of white sun, its gentle rays illuminating her face. A somewhat crooked smile formed, accentuating the small wrinkle around the corner of her mouth, fine as a thin scar. She was so beautiful it sometimes made him ache. She climbed to her feet. "Lead the way, Ranger Rick."

And so he did. They hadn't gone more than twenty feet before the clouds again formed overhead and unleashed great torrents of rain, as cold as ice, another bad omen.

* * *

Despite initially thinking it was going to be impossible, Cortland quickly became accustomed to life in the forest. After his first run-in with a cloud of mosquitos on day two, he'd learned that relative comfort was predicated on thickly applying homemade insect repellent to any and all exposed skin first thing in the morning. The repellent was collected by the natives by smoking birch bark over a metal pan and collecting the tar. The relief it provided was well worth the price of having to go to sleep each night sticky and reeking of smoke.

As promised, Robinson had a few men deliver several heavy boxes of files to Cortland's cottage, the first of many such deliveries. After removing the lid from the first one, which was labeled "Initial Findings" in thick black marker, followed by two dates spanning nearly a month, Cortland discovered countless reams of neatly filed reports and correspondence that Robinson had logged with the Firm. Each sheet of paper was a Xerox of another document—the Firm's logo watermarked at the bottom of each page—and was covered margin to margin with tiny, barely legible print. It was going to be a difficult process, but as he'd learned in school, having too much data to work with was vastly preferable to not having enough.

A week or so passed uneventfully. Cortland ate breakfast at his cabin alone, reviewing paperwork, and shared lunch with Heinrich at Robinson's. There the three men would talk shop. Robinson would fill them in on progress at the crater site, as well as the outlying sites. The platform installation was nearly complete. Pretty soon, they'd have easy access to the crater bottom. At night the men would get together, play cards, and talk about their various paths in life, whatever it was that had brought them here. Cortland, to his credit, did his best to relay his various theories on sentience in everyday objects, about his theory of how objects did not actually exist in time, but rather radiated time from within, gamely answering any questions the others might have. Needless to say, talk of Cortland's work often resulted in jokes about wise-cracking rocks.

Toward the end of this first week, as Cortland received yet another delivery of the Firm's files, Robinson knocked on his door and asked if the two of them could talk. He looked more tired than ever. Cortland invited him in and the two men sat at the kitchen table.

"Please forgive the intrusion," Robinson said. Cortland gestured as if to say it was no intrusion at all and leaned back in his chair. Robinson continued. "When you first arrived here, you asked why, exactly, you'd been summoned. I believe I mentioned that the mining operations had been put on hiatus—and that much is true. However, I'm sure you've noticed that we are still digging. Mr. Cortland, I'm going to request that you take a leap of faith and write a recommendation to the Firm that our digging continues, based on your knowledge of our findings. Would you be willing to comply with this request?" As he spoke, Robinson never once took his eyes off his cup of coffee, which he absentmindedly spun in lazy circles on the table.

"But you haven't told me what these findings are yet. And I haven't come across anything in the files you've provided me with on which to base such a recommendation. I still have no concept of this substance you continually speak of."

Robinson flashed that phosphorescent smile and stood up. "Very well. We will retrieve for you a sample from the crater. And this you will use to conduct the research necessary for your recommendation. It is a dangerous procedure, Mr. Cortland. Yet I am sure Mr. Heinrich will be more than happy to descend into the hole first thing tomorrow morning. In the meantime, please begin drafting your letter. I would like to review it upon its completion." And with that, the small man left, slamming the door behind him.

* * *

Tendrils of mist rose from the crater behind Heinrich as he stood at its edge, his heavy work boots caked with dust. He was silhouetted by the harsh sunlight, and the steel cables that connected his rig to the winches atop the tower crane made him look otherworldly, as if he had grown tubes that fed into some awful machine. As he explained to Cortland, the cables—each of which was half an inch thick and capable of holding some 30,000 pounds—would lower him into the pit. He tugged on his rig, demonstrating its sturdiness. "There's literally a zero percent chance that anything could go wrong," he said. Heinrich pulled a Firm-issued walkie talkie from a holster near his chest and showed Cortland the channel he'd use to relay his progress.

Cortland asked why Heinrich didn't just use the platforms he had so recently—and with such immense effort—installed along the crater wall.

"It's much faster this way," he said. "Just shooting straight down and then coming straight back up. No problems. But in the event that something unforeseen does happen, I'll let you know—just pull me back up to the surface. Only you and Robinson have this channel unlocked. The technicians are on their own channel. In an emergency, Robinson is tasked with notifying them."

"Okay, we'll see you on the other side," Cortland said.

Heinrich smiled at this. "Always." He raised his arm and gave the thumbs up to the tower crane operator.

The unmistakable sound of an industrial generator roared to life. A dozen men climbed onto the rig and took positions near control panels, monitoring the cable feeds and winches. The tower crane rotated on its slewing unit so the jib was positioned directly above the seam. Cortland squinted at the operator's cockpit and saw a blue-shirt return Heinrich's thumbs up, his face occluded by massive headphones, sunglasses, and a walkie mic. With no apparent hesitation, Heinrich repelled backward into the crater, cables taut, one of the mechanical arms attached to the tower crane swiveling minutely to track his movement. The generator drowned out any other sounds, echoed throughout the forest, amplified by the wide valley. Looking at those cables, it was impossible for Cortland not to think of puppets, marionettes. And here approaches the puppet master now, he thought, sighting Robinson as he exited the path from the village.

Cortland saw that a fat black fly was stuck to Robinson's face, just below his eye. And then that familiar, phosphorescent smile wormed into his features, and the fly, disturbed, took off, the slow buzzing of its flight cutting through the air.

Luckily, Robinson did not stop to talk for long. He was here to oversee the descent, he said, raising his voice above the noise. "Have you written your letter of recommendation yet?" Cortland shook his head. Robinson, though visibly disappointed, said nothing in return.

Back in his cabin, Cortland picked up his work where he had left off. The reports were finally getting into the nitty gritty, sort of. Any specific mention of rare earth minerals had been redacted, blacked out, but there were still important documents relating to topography and the tracking of astronomical objects. He listened to the crackle of Heinrich's messages over the walkie talkie. Every ten minutes or so he'd relay an update on his depth coordinates, read his oxygen sensor. They really weren't taking any chances, Cortland thought, once more getting lost in the Firm's files, ream after ream of data: contour line diagrams, geological surveys, aerial and satellite images, and yet so much of it was redacted, the smudged pages Xeroxed and re-Xeroxed into oblivion, that he struggled to make any real sense of the information. Increasingly, the documents did not appear to be arranged in any discernible order: hand-written field notes were followed by endless printouts of data, soil readings, geologic compositions, which were then followed by internal comms reports, all protocol and processes, with names and job titles and charge codes redacted. Even the coordinates on all of the satellite images had been blacked out.

An hour or two of this passed, seemingly with no progress. Cortland's temples throbbed with frustration. Heinrich's transmissions continued crackling on the walkie at regular intervals. Robinson chimed in once or twice, giving the go-ahead to continue the descent.

Cortland felt the whirlwind stress of the past week hit him like a narcotic. He shut his eyes for what felt like the briefest of moments, overcome with fatigue, and was suddenly startled to hear Heinrich cut in on the walkie, shattering the regular rhythm he'd established. "And now the eyes are opening," he said, his voice oddly flat. "I see them now. Eyes in the dust."

At first, Cortland wasn't sure he'd heard correctly. He picked up his walkie and held the talk button. "This is Cortland. Can you repeat that, please? Over." But there was no response, only silence. "Heinrich? Please respond. Over." He waited for Robinson to demand something similar, waited in vain perhaps, because the silence continued unabated. He looked down at the papers before him and saw a typed report signed by Robinson, dated the day before Cortland had arrived. He quickly scanned the text and was dismayed to read that Robinson claimed the mining operations were not only still active, but remarkably successful. There it was, plainly stated—an absolute lie. He flipped to the next page, which was almost solid black. And yet, something was different about this one: it was squirming. The redacted words and sentences crawled over the page like so many black flies. He cried out, threw the papers onto the table in disgust, stood so suddenly that he threw his chair back onto the floor.

For a few moments, Cortland stood there motionless, his pulse pounding in his neck. He waited for something to move, for the flies to emerge and fill the room.

Heinrich's voice, reptilian with static, sounded once more. "They know everything."

Something inside Cortland broke. He didn't even think twice, simply turned, threw open the door of his cottage, and rushed toward the site. He made it about halfway before he came down on an exposed root, actually heard his ankle roll, a wet snapping sound. He tasted dirt as he hit the ground, barely breaking his fall with his elbows. The pain was unbelievable, though it happened in a matter of seconds, and he barely felt any of it. He was back on his feet and limping, thinking only of the sound of Heinrich's voice, the way he sounded so weirdly resigned.

The site came into view, the crater yawning as he fumbled his way down the path, each step rendering the pain more difficult to ignore. Soon enough he saw Robinson, standing near the base of the tower crane. He turned to Cortland as he approached, obviously taken aback by his presence. "Why didn't you say something?" Cortland yelled over the noise of the generator, surprising even himself with how panicked he sounded. He jabbed his finger into Robinson's chest. "Raise him up." The other men gathered around them, grumbling among themselves, seemingly oblivious that anything had gone wrong.

Robinson stared at Cortland blankly, then licked his lips. "You're covered in dirt, you know. Like a worm." Then he slowly raised his walkie to his lips and quietly gave the command to raise Heinrich. The winches set in motion. "He went down there at your command," Robinson said. Cortland ignored him, turned his attention to the crater, waited. The wait felt endless. And then Heinrich's rig emerged from the pit, empty, but otherwise undisturbed, as if he'd simply slipped through it and fallen into oblivion.

* * *

Robinson stormed off to his cottage, where he claimed he was not to be disturbed. Cortland, at Robinson's insistence, was carried back to the village on a stretcher by two blue-shirts, his ankle now swollen to twice its normal size. The pain was nearly unbearable, worsened by the grief and confusion he felt over Heinrich's inexplicable disappearance.

The blue-shirts took Cortland to some sort of unofficial clinic—a two-room shed that had been outfitted with beds and cabinets filled with medical supplies—where, he quickly realized, he was expected to wrap his own ankle. Cortland retrieved the supplies he needed and sat down on one of the beds. He took a few Tylenol 3s, hoping in vain that they'd be strong enough to curb the pain. The blue-shirts stood on either side of the door, watching him closely. He recognized them: the one with the twisted lip, the other with the gold ring. "You're the same men from before," he said, tearing off a strip of bandage with his teeth. "You tended to the man in Robinson's cottage—the one with the insect bite." The men exchanged a brief look. "Sure," one of them said, "whatever you say."

Just as Cortland finished tightening the compression wrap around his ankle, securing it in place with metal fasteners, his walkie talkie crackled to life and Robinson's voice came through. "Once you've dressed your injuries, report to my cottage."

A few minutes of painful hobbling later, the blue-shirts keeping close watch over him, Cortland pushed through Robinson's door and saw the principal sitting at his table, a .45 handgun before him. He looked surprisingly calm, though the colorlessness of his lips, the way his eyes darted from one thing to the next, betrayed worry. "How idiotic can you be?"

"Do you really think that's an appropriate tone to take with me?" Cortland said. He sat down opposite Robinson, propping up his bad ankle on the next chair. "Especially…" He searched for the right words. "Considering the circumstances?"

"Heinrich is dead," Robinson said, as if it were a mere matter of fact. "There is no use being indirect with our language. We must be precise. There are problems that need to be immediately dealt with, Mr. Cortland. One word of advice: never, ever reveal that something is amiss before the natives. You should have let me handle that situation. You have no understanding of the damage you've done. They believe a god has been disturbed, that we have set upon a path to destruction. I told you they were a superstitious people—fatalists—a most dangerous quality when combined with fear." The look on his face suddenly softened. He closed his eyes as if in meditation. "Please, let's not bicker. Not now. It's unprofessional. And we have much work to do."

"That's why you need the gun?" Cortland said, nodding to the handgun on the table. It was solid black and looked immensely heavy.

"When it's called for, of course. It's the natives, they're restless. My liaison has betrayed us, I'm sure of it. Earlier today he and some of the others gathered in the woods beyond the site. They held a clandestine meeting. He is telling lies. He's recruiting. I fear we have lost even more men to the paranoia. He spreads it like a disease. We are dealing with it. I fear for my safety. There have already been threats. Things at the site are chaotic, tense."

"What are you going to do?"

"It's no matter." Robinson cast his eyes toward the table. "If things do really go south, we have a failsafe plan we can put in motion—but only as a last resort. A last resort that you can ensure we avoid. After all, we brought you here from quite a distance, at great expense. I've given you all the paperwork you requested, all of the facts, the research. It's time for you to hold up your end of the agreement."

"Agreement?"

"You need to write the letter of recommendation to the Firm," Robinson said, talking through his teeth. "Too much time has already been wasted. The letter must be sent immediately. I've arranged for a pickup. A boat will arrive any minute now. You must tell them what we are dealing with in the crater. And you must promise that it will bring about an entirely new industry."

"But I don't even know that. How could I? I haven't learned anything since I've been here. The whole time there's been one obfuscation after another."

"That's unacceptable." Robinson slumped in his seat and rubbed each of his temples with two fingers. "Most unacceptable."

"Why are you reporting to the Firm that the mining operations for the precious minerals are still active? You said yesterday that they had been delayed indefinitely. You're lying to them, stringing them along. Why?"

Robinson laughed quietly then emitted an odd, high-pitched whining sound. He shut his eyes, his open mouth a rictus of frustration, impatience. He raised the gun up over head and shook it, a gesture that, perhaps as intended, made him look totally unhinged. "Included that in the files, did I? I'm sure you understand the difficulty. Creating the paperwork for an entire team of consultants has been difficult. I haven't had much sleep at all."

"Why? Why did you do this? Why did you go to all this trouble?"

"Isn't it obvious? Do you really think the Firm would continue to fund this operation of ours if they knew what we were really doing here? I've been buying time, giving them the numbers necessary to maintain our funding. Everything they wanted to hear. All the while, I knew we were getting closer to something that the world had never before imagined possible—unfettered communication. Tapping into the vacuous realm. Don't you see? I didn't understand any of it until I read your work. *The Nonhuman Turn.* There are…things down there at the bottom of that crater that are smarter than anything we could possibly imagine. They communicate without using language. They've moved beyond what we know as consciousness. We will harness their intelligence and use it to great benefit. The Firm will grow rich beyond any previous understanding of the word. I will be valorized, promoted to global director. The world will save untold amounts of money. The environment will restabilize. Don't you see, Mr. Cortland? We can save the world. We can save all of humankind from its inevitable extinction."

Cortland was dumbstruck. He fumbled for words, to make any sort of response—didn't even know where to start, really. "What sorts of *things* are in the crater?"

"When I first arrived here in the forest, I learned that I suffered from a deathly fear of insects, of bugs, spiders, millipedes, anything with more than four legs. Simply stumbling across one of these creatures in my cabin or out on the trail would result in my total paralysis. Such a fear placed me in a rather difficult position, considering their ubiquity." He emphasized the individual syllables of this last word, spitting out each one with contempt. "Forget being mauled by a bear. At least then you have the luxury of dying quickly, relatively speaking. But have you ever seen what the bite of a Karakurt spider can do to a man when hospitalization is not an option? Can you imagine the horror of fresh maggots as they emerge from a man's open wounds? I have seen both of those things—saw them on my very first day here, no less. I soon realized that these creatures inhabit a realm entirely not our own, something you yourself have referred to as the vacuous realm in your writings, the space that seeks only to be filled. A shared, immediate intelligence. This is the nature of the universe, is it not? A hole opens up—somewhere, some place—and pulls in everything that surrounds it. Well, what we have here is a hole, and I believe that it is pulling in our very consciousness. That it is feeding off of us. And that we, in turn, have no choice but to become part of its great black mind. And that in doing so, we can learn from it. Become it."

"What you're saying is insane."

"Let's not be so reductive. You of all people should be more open minded. They speak to me. They've given me great visions of the way things will come to be beyond time. The beyond itself is a fold within a black dream. You too will come to understand, Mr. Cortland, once you see the eyes in the dust."

Cortland remembered what Heinrich said, just before his transmissions went silent. *I see them now. Eyes in the dust.* Robinson had clearly been driven mad by the immensity and remoteness of the woods, powerful fears he was helpless to control, and theories he couldn't quite grasp. There was no other explanation. It had all coalesced into some kind of sick, twisted fantasy.

"Don't look at me like that," Robinson said, "with pity in your eyes. You think you understand. You think you know better. But you don't. You are a worm. And it's going to swallow all of us, all of this." He gestured around the room, waving the gun wildly. "I alone can keep it at bay, keep it satisfied. In exchange, we will be granted access to its knowledge. And this knowledge will bring all aspects of life into tune. Surely, you've heard them, Mr. Cortland? The sound of their humming at night? The sound of the fabric of all things? Isn't it joyous?"

An almost unspeakable black horror fell all around Cortland, a veil obscuring any previous understanding of the way things were. Robinson was right; he hadn't even realized it until now. The sound of the humming, the wall of noise. It had long ago melded with his consciousness, tentacles laced through his brainwaves.

"I can see it on your face. You *do* know what I'm talking about. You know all too well. But we need more time. More resources. You must do what I have commanded. It will buy us time. Time is what's most important here. And I fear that we are running dangerously low on this, our most valuable commodity. Now go and do not return unless you have written that fucking letter."

* * *

It was midday—the white sun scorching in the empty sky—and the village was eerily quiet. Most of the cottages had shuttered their windows. Cortland limped his way back toward his cabin, his ankle throbbing, the pain radiated throughout his entire body, causing even his teeth to ache. The few locals he passed along the way avoided his eyes, didn't bother with returning his sheepish greetings. There didn't seem to be any blue-shirts around. In the village square, he saw the young boy in the T-shirt who had greeted him on his first morning at the site. "Hey," he called out, trying his best to sound anything other than scared. "Remember me?" The boy didn't even look in Cortland's direction, simply turned and fled, the soft thudding of his bare feet on the forest floor bleeding into the rustling of branches as he disappeared into the surrounding woods. Cortland kept on, sucking air through his teeth. Another man, an older native who sat on the ground near the risers, actually snarled at him as he passed, lashed out with a claw-like hand. Cortland barely maneuvered beyond the old man's reach, the sudden movement causing white-hot explosions of pain throughout his leg. The smell of vodka on the man's breath was unmistakable; his half-open eyes looked yellowed and lethargic.

A flash of yellow in the distance caught his eye. At first he thought, really tried his damnedest to believe, that it was anything else, maybe an exotic bird, or even the sun, the way it so often seemed to glimmer through the trees. But that was just wishful thinking. He knew it was wishful thinking, the mechanism of his mind, trying to protect him from… From what? From seeing the impossible? Because what he saw was definitely impossible. The yellow he saw was a dull, mustardy yellow, the yellow of a rain jacket. *Her* rain jacket.

Up until now, Cortland hadn't actually let himself believe that he might be losing his mind. But as he heard himself call out Claire's name, his voice shrill and not at all familiar, not like his voice at all; as he tasted his salty, hot tears; as he crunched down on his ankle again and again and again, he realized that he had probably lost it, was at least sufficiently self-aware enough to know this.

The magnificent trees of the forest enveloped him, darkening the sky, the hot smell of decay filling his senses. Seconds later he came to a small, circular clearing filled with tall ferns, which he parted with his hands as he continued on. Equipment littered the ground and, beyond the center of the clearing, the reinforced entrance to a darkened tunnel emerged from the ground. This must have been one of the satellite sites Robinson had mentioned.

As he made his way toward the tunnel entrance, Cortland nearly stumbled into a knee-deep pit. And in that pit he saw dozens of gray, lifeless bodies thrown in a heap on top of one another. They'd been stripped of their clothing, some missing limbs, others their heads. The smell was like nothing he had ever encountered before, sweet and rotten at the same time, like apples left out in the sun. And there, on top of the others, was the body of the man he'd seen on his very first day at the site, the one who had been bitten by an insect, injected with something, disappeared from Robinson's cabin. The body had been laid on its back, arms curled tight against the chest in rigor mortis, mouth offset and open. The eyes were gone and a thick centipede emerged from one of the blackened cavities, slid up and around the curve of the skull, its many clicking legs digging into what remained of his blue-gray skin.

Cortland fell onto his hands and knees and threw up, heaving, felt it all come out in one great blackened rope of scabby tissue and yellow bile. His vomit hit the ground and instantly fractured into hundreds of shiny black beetles. The bugs scattered into the recesses of the clearing, racing toward the mouth of the tunnel where they disappeared into the black.

He knew now that she had led him here, Claire had, so that he might learn the truth, in case he had any lingering doubts as to Robinson's monstrous nature. He curled into a ball in the dirt. He was never going home. He would die in these woods. No one who came to Robinson's site ever left, not really. Even the lucky ones, the ones who passed quickly, never fully understanding the sheer magnitude of discovery awaiting those left behind, they were merely absorbed into an endless stretch of cosmic decay.

He felt the first stirrings of everything coming undone, the encroaching black of the hole eating away at the edges of his mind, the vacuous realm, everywhere and nowhere. He rolled onto his back and stared into the sky. The white sun trembled, ringed by dozens of crooked black flares, viscous and gleaming, yet swaying rhythmically, weightless like smoke. This was the knowledge: that death was not an exit, but rather a succumbing to the great black folds, those streams of utter ruin that rained down from the spaces between the stars in spidery arcs, falling upon the world and mercilessly wiping it away in all its impermanence, little more than a putrid sprinkling of dust on a quaking bed of volcanic rock.

Cortland shut his eyes and welcomed the all-knowing black as it closed in upon him.

* * *

The bear cave was little more than a narrow, crooked passage, and must have been formed millions of years ago when the much larger slabs of granite that made up its angled walls first slid into place. They crouched at its entrance for a minute or two, listening. The smell emanating from the cave's depths was overpowering and earthy. Satisfied that it was unoccupied, Claire shone the strobe into its misty blackness. Gently trickling rivulets of water streamed along the cave walls. Clumps of spongy brown mushrooms sprouted all along the floor.

"I'm gonna go in," she said. Cortland's face must have shown his concern, because she quickly added, "Not too far. Just want to see what it's like. I've never been this close to an actual bear cave before."

The rain was coming down harder than ever, great big drops, splashing on the rocks, a wash of white noise crackling like so much static. At this point, Cortland's slicker had soaked through and the cold had seeped into his skin. His teeth actually chattered as he told Claire to be careful, to not go in too deep.

It was a moment he played and replayed in his memory over and over again, all these years later, a nightmare reel stuck on an endless loop. He watched helplessly as Claire entered the mouth of the cave, still crouching, carefully inching along the sloping ground, the echoing sound of her boots squeaking against the wet rocks. She pressed her hand against the wall to help her balance, cradled the strobe in her free arm, its beam waving erratically. And then the darkness of the cave seemed to swallow her whole—her bright yellow raincoat disappearing in an instant—leaving in her place nothing but swirling darkness and mist. He heard the unmistakable sound of the strobe's bulb shattering, a soft crunch, impossibly far away.

"Claire?" he called out. "Claire, are you alright?"

The sound of the rain pounding on the surrounding rocks seemed to intensify, a frantic, rhythmic percussion. What if she had been hurt? She could be calling out to him for help and he wouldn't be able to hear her.

He called out her name once more, his pulse quickening in his throat. He ducked under the entrance to the cave. And then her voice, or something like her voice, a low tortured groan, coming up from deep below. How had she gone in so deep so quickly?

Cortland got down on his hands and knees and felt along the ground, quickly confirmed his worst fears: the floor of the cave abruptly gave way to a steep ledge, the rain waters flowing over the slippery edge in a steady stream, pouring into what sounded like a shallow pool some ten feet below. It was too dark to see anything. He called into the blackness.

"I'm here," Claire said. "I…hit my head. Freezing. My leg."

What happened next remained in Cortland's memory only as a blur of panic and frustration. There was no way he could have gotten down to her, no way that he could have done anything other than what he did. So why did he still blame himself after all these years? Why did he still feel like he could have saved her if he had only been smart enough, or strong enough to figure it out? Dammit, why hadn't he been able to figure it out?

It took him an hour to get back down to the bottom of the bluff, another thirty minutes to get to his Jeep, which had sunk even deeper into the mud. By the time he'd managed to get out onto a main road, flag down a passerby, get on their phone and call for help, another thirty minutes had passed. The sun had gone down and the woods were freezing as he led the rescue team back up to the glacial moraine. And the sun was rising by the time they lifted her out of that cave, the long-awaited end of a thousand-year storm.

She'd been dead for more than twelve hours.

* * *

God knows how much time passed as Cortland lay on his back in that clearing in the woods. The sky above him twirled sickeningly in a time lapse, the light of the stars blurring into glowing arcs of light, as if the world turned one way, the sky the other.

He heard Claire's voice beckon to him, filling him with warmth. "You can still save me," she said. "I'm still right here where you left me. I'm down here at the bottom of this hole." He felt the pain in his ankle melt away, a sudden wave of strength fill his limbs. Her voice was inside him, filling him. "Come and look deep within yourself, look down and deep. The eyes will open for you."

The path back to the village was lined with hundreds of ghastly figures, their skin sloughing from their faces, eyes hollow and obsidian. Among them Cortland recognized the unblinking visage of Heinrich, though the other man made no such human connection. The gaunt specters turned slowly as Cortland passed by, slowly raising their arms and extending their fingers, pointing him in the direction he knew he must travel, toward the center of all things.

Robinson's body—Cortland knew it as such, despite the fact that its face had been degloved—hung suspended by ropes in the birch archway that marked the entrance to the village, a steaming slush of his entrails pooled on the ground. Placed at the base of each post, like sentinels, were the lifeless corpses of Robinson's two most trusted men: the one with the twisted lip, the other with the gold ring. Their hands had been tied behind their backs, their eyes removed. The old man, Robinson's liaison, stood in the archway, blocking Cortland's path. As Cortland approached, he too stepped aside and raised an arm, pointing. Cortland ducked beneath the gory spectacle, made his way through the village, and then down the path that led into Purgatory Gulch.

There stood the unmovable formations of Heaven and Hell, black against the pulsing, electric sky. The whole valley was lit with the power of a thousand stars. The two great stones were a gateway to the beyond, Cortland understood that now. The tower crane rig was gone; in its place stood nothing, a gaping, formidable crag, as if the bedrock surrounding the crater had given way, pulling down the machinery with it, disappearing it into the earth.

Cortland heard the hum, the sound that Robinson had once referred to as the fabric of all things, and knew now that it was emanating from the hole. He listened closely, heard within its drone infinite patterns, genius designs beyond his wildest dreams.

"You always said that once you whittled away all the lies—the illusions—there was only being at its most pure—pure and without thought."

"Claire?" he said. He felt tears streaming down his face, felt the hurt open up, such a deep hole within, aching. He climbed the sharp metal steps that led to the platform system, his boots sounding out loudly on the steel with each step, echoing down into the pit.

"I'm here," she said. Her voice was beautiful, exactly as he had remembered it. "Come to me and our thoughts will be one."

Time compressed itself into an instant as he made his way down the series of steps and platforms, stretched out once more as he reached the very last platform, its edges licking at the black below. He climbed up onto the steel-beam railing, leaning forward slightly over the abyss. There was no question of belief; things simply were the way they were. He had always known this to be true, an irrefutable fact.

From deep within the swirling black of the pit, Cortland watched as a spot of light hatched in the darkness, a tiny gleam of silver. Moments later, there was another speck of light, and then another. Within the span of a few seconds, thousands more appeared, blinking open in the inky black, all pulling together into a spiral, slowly spinning around a single point, a black disc ringed by blue and purple clouds. The disc slipped away, leaving in its place a hole, a vacuum that needed to be filled, sucking the spiraling clouds downward, their folds lined with the glimmering spots of light, all spinning together so quickly now.

There she was, Claire, at the bottom of the bear cave. The water from the ledge above showered down upon her, splashed against his yellow raincoat. Her leg was broken, angled oddly. She had pulled back her hood so he could clearly see her face.

"I knew you wouldn't leave me here," she said, extending her hand.

Cortland reached out to her—she wasn't nearly as far away as he had remembered—only registering too late that her voice was not her voice, but the voice of something ancient and greatly displeased. A shadow snaked up from the pit, falling upon him. He was plucked effortlessly from that platform and pulled down into the depths. There was no sensation of falling. Instead, it was as if his body was being carried up into the sky, an endless void stretching up and outward into a perfect cone, the final passage before he could begin a new life among the secretive stars. Such was his last thought before his mortal body was separated into all its various elements, shot outward and all at once into the universe in as many directions as were physically possible.

PUBLICATION HISTORY

"Helping Hands" originally published in *Pank* (2009).

"Out of Step in the Kingdom of Our Lord" originally published in *the Collagist* (2016).

"House of Abjection" originally published in *Nightscript* (2017) and anthologized in *Year's Best Weird Fiction Volume Five* (Undertow Publications, 2018).

"Phantoms" originally published in *Juked* (2016).

"The Final Diagnosis of Doctor Lazare" originally published in *Twice-Told: A Collection of Doubles* (Chthonic Matter, 2019).

"Dreams from the Darklands" originally published as a chapbook by Mud Luscious Press (2010).

"Stargazer" is original to this collection.

"The Schoolmaster" originally published in *Nox Pareidolia* (Nightscape Press, 2019).

"The Gutter at the Bottom of the World" originally published in *Pluto in Furs* (Plutonian Press, 2019).

"Dead Babies" originally published in *the Fanzine* (2019).

"King of the Rats" originally published in *Wigleaf* (2011).

"Strange Signals from the Center of the Earth" originally published in *Glowing in the Dark* (Aqueous Books, 2012).

"Eyes in the Dust" originally published as a novelette by Dunhams Manor Press (2016).

ABOUT THE AUTHOR

DAVID PEAK is the author of *Corpsepaint* (Word Horde, 2018) and *The Spectacle of the Void* (Schism, 2014). He lives in Chicago.

CPSIA information can be obtained
at www.ICGtesting.com
Printed in the USA
BVHW070030250321
603354BV00006B/65